FLAG 9
A.G. RIVES

For my parents, who gave me a love of learning
and the discipline to get things done.

Acknowledgments

Without my dear Margaret Fishback, I may have never boarded the *Hannah Cole,* or written about a guy named Drew Mcfarland sailing aboard her. You enhance my life as you have enhanced this work with your talent. I would like to also thank Marilyn Spiller, my editor, for coping with a Zombie novel that started out as a culmination of text messages to myself, emails, and a variety of other chicken scratch. Special thanks to the welcoming staff at Fort Clinch, Amelia Island. If you ever get a chance to visit, make sure you do-they are very gracious about taking people in. To the Ritz-Carlton, Amelia Island, my apologies for the damage to your building. Please send the bill to Carlos. For everyone else who supported me in this endeavor, I thank you. Lastly, hat off to all Biomedical Field Service Engineers and those that support them.

Author's Note

It was a phone call with my girlfriend Margaret and an episode of AMC's *The Walking Dead* (pick any one) that set Drew on his journey. "I'm going to write a Zombie book," I announced as we said goodnight (sure you will, she was probably thinking). Setting the phone down, I opened my laptop and stared at the stark whiteness of a fresh Microsoft Word document.

My motivation wasn't any particular episode of that miniseries but the culmination of all the genre books, movies, and TV shows that I had enjoyed since I was a kid. I remember looking forward to a local access show that came on every Saturday, Commander USA's *Groovy Movies*. It came on after cartoons. What you got was a pair of the worst horror thrillers produced, hosted by a middle aged dad in a superhero outfit that did magic tricks during commercial breaks. I couldn't get enough and just like my love of candy has never changed, neither has my interest in creepy stories.

That being said, I set out to do something a little different in a new environment. I wanted to freshen up the genre with a tale of a disrupted solo-circumnavigation attempt. At first, I tried to guide Drew, but ultimately he was the one that took me on a trip. For that, I am in his debt.

My hope is that you enjoy reading this as much as I enjoyed writing it. Thank you.

Chapter 1

The 1966 Alberg 35 lolled calmly, some 90 nautical miles off the coast of Charleston, South Carolina. As the sun was coming over the horizon, it formed the color banding of a periwinkle shell within the distant clouds. Drew McFarland threw the lanyard of a battered green set of West Marine binoculars around his neck and grabbed his portable VHF. Securing a handrail, he made quick exit up the steps and through the varnished teak companionway of the *SV Hannah Cole*. The morning breeze was just picking up as he made his way up to the deck and scanned the skyline through the haze of salt smeared lenses for the 37 foot Island Packet.

There she laid in bare poles about a half a mile away, her cream hull standing out against the November sky. Nobody appeared to be on deck but it was difficult to tell from this distance.

Drew checked the squelch and placed the VHF to chapped lips.

"*Sailing vessel Owl of Athena*, this is the *Hannah Cole*. Do you copy?"

Drew throttled off the Standard Horizon and paused to listen.

There was no response.

Checking Squelch again, *"Owl of Athena* this is the *Hannah Cole*, over."

Still, silence.

"Jack, Dottie, pick up the damned radio, over!"

There was only crack from the small speaker, then silence all but for the whistle of the breeze between the handheld and Drew's sunburned ear.

Stepping back into the cockpit, Drew lifted the glow plug switch for a second and turned the key, awakening the 25xp Universal diesel. *Hannah* vibrated and then settled into a smooth rumble as he took hold of the shift lever and eased it forward. As always, the "Chitty-Chitty-Bang-Bang" song from Walt Disney's crew popped into his head as the diesel warmed up and smoothed out.

Drew began his journey over to the *Owl of Athena*.

It was supposed to have been a three day shakedown cruise. Then, it was to be an adventure off the edge of the mainland. A lot drunk, the idea had come to him one night nearly two years after a man named George Clarke simply forgot to latch his tandem jet-ski trailer down properly and it came loose on I-95. Careening into the side of Drew's wife Hannah's Dodge Grand Caravan, the multi-car accident that ensued killed her and their four year old child, Cole.

Drew was crushing beers at Big Johns Tavern on East Bay Street in Charleston with Stephen Meese, an old sailing friend, sailboat rigger, and now fellow alcoholic. The once handsome Meese had the drugs, smoking, and two divorces by forty, showing their signs of wear. Drew, sitting across from him was no mirror image. At six feet tall he had retained his strong physique and handsome features despite his lack of sleep and long nights at the bottle. He also showed little interest in the women at the table next to them that had been admiring his brown eyes and disheveled sandy blonde hair. In Drew's mind he wasn't on the market.

"Drew-Mack-Foo, I have known you for a while and hate to see you like this," Stephen said, as they closed the tab and got up from the table. "You need to at least get out of the house and have a sail. It's been over two years."

"A sail will fix all my woes, huh?" Drew questioned, bracing himself against the table as he stood.

"Look, tomorrow, meet me at C dock. We are putting a new Selden boom on a Beneteau 42 and taking her out for a shake down. I know you're not doing anything but sitting around in your own misery-so no excuses," Stephen said, putting his arm around Drew's shoulder as the two staggered through the doorway of the bar into the rain swept street.

Stephen put on the pressure, "Promise to be there 9 AM, Drew. I know it will be a rough getting your ass in gear considering the state you are in now, but a good sail will make a new man of you. You got to get back on that horse."

"I will do you one better. I will buy a boat and sail it around the world, my friend," Drew said, pointing a drunken finger with crazed emphasis at the disinterested clouds that passed overhead.

"Sure you will big man," Stephen said, patting his equally drunk friend on the back before trekking a windy path back to Drew's house on Bull Street.

Stephen had been right. Being out on the water again had caused a stir in Drew's heart and his conscience. He had seen challenges once more that were long forgotten in misery. He saw opportunities that could make him feel alive again and obstacles that could potentially threaten a life he no longer had interest in living. He needed to feel like he had something to lose. He owed it to the wife and child he had loved so dearly to do something, anything.

"So, Mack-Foo, you still gonna sail around the world?" Stephen called, as he walked the windward gunnel out to the bow where Drew was managing headsails. The 42 foot Beneteau, *Heart Break Hotel,* was tacking homeward after a magnificent day's sail in steady 18 knot winds.

Drew looked back at his approaching shipmate and nodded, "I think I will."

Things after that had gone by fast, a blur. Within six months his small two-story on Bull Street sold, giving him 32k in equity. He was also financially secure due to the million from his wife's life insurance settlement which had already allowed him to quit his job as a biomedical engineer, stay drunk all the time, and still manage to pay the light bill.

After weeks of research, he bought a mint condition 1966 Alberg 35 and for her sea worthiness as well as appearance, the *Hannah Cole* was a swan of a yacht. For the next year he lived aboard and conducted a full refit with no expense spared. It became his new addiction, the new drug, as his alcohol days dwindled and then petered out. From late nights at the bar, it became late nights in the books and hanging with the old salts at the pier.

In the Charleston City Marina, two of these old salts were Jack and Dorothy Potter – an older, retired couple in their mid-sixties on a heavily outfitted Island Packet berthed next to *Hannah*. Jack previously owned a successful VW dealership and Dottie was a retired school teacher. They mostly traveled up and down the intercostal waterway and to the Bahamas on occasion but had always wanted to venture further. Because of that desire, they made close friends with their slip mate on *Hannah* and joined as escort on several ocean trials during Drew's preparation. They wore it on their sleeves that they were living vicariously through him.

Drew waited until November, after hurricane season, for a three day sea trial before heading south toward a new life; Jack and Dottie once again, had agreed to come along as escort. They were a day and a half into the trip and 80 nautical miles offshore when their vessels first received the radio chatter.

"This is the United States Coast Guard, sector Charleston SC, all vessels are reminded to monitor channel 16 for further information concerning the events unfolding in Charleston and surrounding counties. We ask that channel 16 be kept clear for all further updates."

Switching to Weather-WX, "…seas 2-3 feet, skies clear, winds 5-8 knots. All vessels are asked to monitor channel 16 for information concerning developments on the unidentified infection spreading rapidly across the Southeast. All residents of South Carolina and surrounding states are asked to remain inside their homes and not approach anyone displaying suspicious behavior. Your best course of action is to remain inside your homes and monitor channel 16 for more information."

It took only 45 minutes of the same looped message from first radio contact until the Standard Horizon broadcast nothing but silence on channel 16. It was two hours later that the WX channel issued its last statement.

There had been no further updates from either frequency.

Jack came over the radio sarcastically, "Infection? Shit, I must have forgotten to flush the toilet back at the marina."

Drew figured Captain Morgan had been first mate on the Owl since early that morning because Jack sounded pretty hammered.

Drew pictured Dottie rolling her eyes as she took the handheld from Jack. Her voice had a bit more sense of urgency, "Andrew, we don't need to be going back to Charleston. We have plenty of supplies and fuel to get a bit down the coast, maybe Savannah. I don't know about you boys but that's where I'm headed, even if I have to take the dinghy, over."

In the background, Drew could hear their tri-color, longhaired Chihuahua, Bella, barking. Jack was trying to shut her up.

"I know Dottie, but we have not heard anything more from the Coast Guard or any other channel for that matter," Drew said, getting caught midsentence before he heard the low rumble of jets approaching. He peered out of the cabin to see a formation of F/A-18s flying westbound, toward Charleston.

All arguments with Dottie ended there.

"You won't have to twist our arms, Dottie. I think we are both in agreement with you," Drew conceded, dropping the handheld VHF to his side and staring up at the jet trails that left white claw scratches in the sky.

Both parties radioed off and on that night, and agreed to go silent at 10PM in order to be rested for a trip toward Savannah in the morning. There was not much sleep to be had as Drew spent his time going over boat provisions in order to draw mental focus from the possible events unfolding back home. What had happened? What were they facing now?

Drew cursed himself for not getting luxuries like satellite TV or any entertainment for that matter.

"Would have been nice to know what the fuck was going on back in the states, you dumbass," he muttered to himself. Jack and Dottie were not any better off as they had always been perfectly satisfied with their tube TV/VHS combo bungee corded to a shelf in their salon. That's what old sailors did-high technology, like sextants.

It was 2 AM when Drew finally lay exhausted in *Hannah*'s v-birth when he heard what sounded like thunder rumbling in the distance. Through a cabin deadlight, an orange glow lit up the darkness over Charleston. He did not need to see the news to know that there had been a tremendous event.

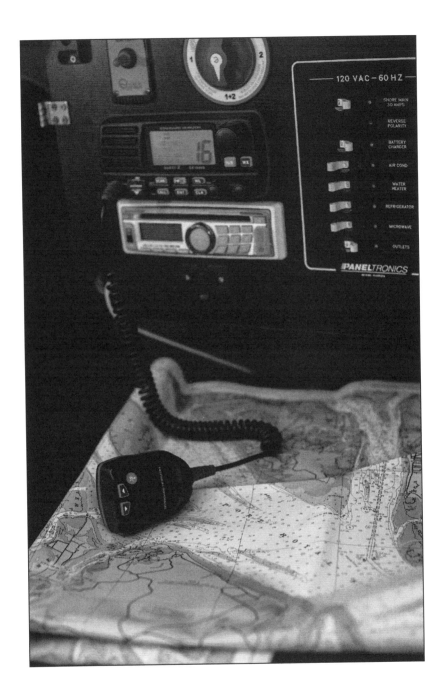

Chapter 2

The sun sat a little higher in the sky and the breeze died off by the time Drew had *Hannah* close enough to notice that the business end of the Jack and Dottie's dinghy was in the water while its bow was still dangling from the *Owl*'s davits.

Drew made his approach from the south and gently guided *Hannah* around the *Owl*'s stern to her starboard side. From this angle he was close enough to see two stanchions amidships that had been torn free from their mounts and dangled uselessly from the lifelines they once supported.

Drew had a sinking, troubled feeling as he tried the radio again.

"Jack, Dottie, this is Drew, approaching you to starboard, over."

Nothing.

Switching to 69, he tried the frequency, "Jack, Dottie, pickup! Is everything alright?"

Drew kept trying until he was close enough in range to the *Owl* that he could hear the sound of his own growing distress as his voice echoed back from their radio.

They hear me loud and clear, he thought. Buy why

haven't they..?

Drew caught his eye on a figure emerging from the companionway door. With her silver hair pulled back into the familiar ponytail and the powder blue Helly Hansen coastal jacket, Drew recognized Dottie immediately.

"Dottie, thank God," Drew said, easing *Hannah* 10 feet alongside the *Owl*'s gunwale.

She turned and spotted him.

Locking eyes with Dottie, Drew immediately recoiled, tangling his legs in the tiller. He fell back hard against *Hannah*'s cockpit bench. "Jesus Christ," he yelled on his way down.

He had seen a face like that before during his four year tour in the Military. It was in the Air Force basic training gas chamber. You entered the chamber with your gas mask on. The drill instructor would pop a canister and you were to take your mask off and exit the building. Once outside, you would join your fellow wretching recruits in a frenzy of snot, hacking, coughing, and bloodshot eyes. He remembered it being like someone had opened all the floodgates of his head. That was Dottie now.

Adrenaline hit with an uppercut, slamming him into fight -or-flight mode. It was a half a second before his hand was again on the throttle lever, surging *Hannah* forward in the water.

Dottie erupted from the cockpit screaming a shrill cry of madness and pain as she scrambled the length of the *Owl*'s gunwale, lashing out in a rage as *Hannah* passed to starboard.

"Holy fuck, holy fuck, holy fuck," Drew said in a rapid succession that syncopated with his out of control heart rate.

Drew jerked his head around to make eye contact with Dottie again as he crossed in front of the *Owl*'s bow.

"Dottie, it's me," he called out, hoping to calm her apparent anger with him. What's her deal? he thought. The radio had mentioned people acting suspiciously and this was certainly suspicious.

"Dottie, what's going on?"

She didn't respond.

"It's me, Drew," he yelled, pleading.

Dottie reached the bow pulpit and Drew could see blood down her front and blackening in her teeth as her lips pulled back inhumanly tight before she let out another scream.

The sound was a defibrillator on Drew's nervous system and it was cranked to 360 joules. He could feel his vision tunneling as the bow of the *Hannah* stretched out to the horizon as if it wanted to get there quicker than the stern.

Dottie let out another wail, destroying her own vocal cords.

Drew ducked at the change in tone as if dodging an invisible blow.

The next attempt left a sound like gargling, all air, giving way to a loud throat clearing sound, a croaking.

As Drew throttled forward, the universal's ponies were at full gallop trying to overcome *Hannah*'s full keel.

At 50 yards he cut the engine, grabbed the binoculars and dashed up onto the deck next to the mast as *Hannah* settled in her own wake.

What the hell just happened? Drew thought, panting to catch his breath. She is acting like she doesn't recognize me.

Raising the binoculars, he focused in on the *Owl*.

Dottie remained at the bow, rocking side to side, staring at the sea, staring at Drew, a tiger in a cage, trying to reach her prey, trying to find a way over the liquid gap between them. Despite the distance, Drew didn't want to keep his eyes off her as if she may actually find a way across. What the fuck is wrong with her? Why is she after me?

With frayed nerves, he returned to the cockpit and picked up the handheld VHF.

Channel 16, checking squelch, "Mayday, mayday, United States Coast Guard, this is the *SV Hannah Cole*. We have a medical emergency. I repeat, we have a med..."

Drew stopped and placed the handheld back in its mount. If this is what the people looked like back home-anything like what had taken place back home-it was probably best to not give away his position. After all, the Coast Guard had issued their last message hours ago.

With that, Drew went below into the cabin, turned off his AIS, returned to the cockpit, and stared out at the woman that prowled back and forth on the bow of the *Owl of Athena*. She was keeping watch on his every movement.

Drew had learned early in his professional life that it was important to gather data before making any major decisions as long as you weren't just making excuses to procrastinate. A million questions now flooded his brain. Where was Jack? Hell, where was the damn dog? Oh, and the blood on Dottie's jacket drying brown against the nylon? What of that? He had just spoken with her the night before. Was she sick with whatever this was they were talking about on the radio? Did Jack get sick? Is that what was happening here?

Drew faced westward toward Charleston as if to see answers on the horizon. Is it happening everywhere?

One thing Drew was certain of, some of these questions needed to be answered before he was to make any major decision and he could possibly find some of them aboard the *Owl of Athena.*

He formulated a plan.

It was getting late in the afternoon when the sea and the sky had merged together with the same silver hue until there was only a hint of horizon left. The wind vane at the top of *Hannah*'s mast swiveled back and forth as if trying to pick a direction and couldn't make up its mind. The air speed meter loped along at 2 knots and the relatively flat sea told the same tale. Now was the time to go.

Drew released *Hannah*'s dinghy lines and his little inflatable settled into the sea.

Looking out toward the Owl, he lifted the VHF handheld to his mouth and spoke, "Dottie, come down here. I'm down here, Dottie."

Dottie spun wildly at the sound of the voice she heard from below and raced back to the cockpit. Sticking her head in the companionway, she searched the *Owl*'s cabin.

Finding nothing, she brought her fury back out to the bow and focused again on her business with the *Hannah Cole.*

Drew grabbed two 50 foot coils of line, an extra life jacket, the handheld radio, and stepped into his dinghy.

Smoke erupted from the little 6hp Nissan as he pulled its starter rope and it sputtered alive. He could see its commotion was driving Dottie into another fit. It was almost like she (the anxious hostess) understood someone was coming for a visit. She waited impatiently as Drew cut through the water toward her.

At a distance of 40 feet, with Dottie lashing out even more vigorously, Drew throttled off and prepared to initiate his plan. Taking the two coils of rope, he tied them together and fastened the extra life jacket at the junction. At one end of the rope he fastened a bowline, making the loop large enough to easily secure purchase. Starting at the bow he began to make his pass around the *Owl of Athena*. Crossing around the starboard side, he triggered the handheld and made his call.

"Dottie, come around back here," he coaxed. "Come to the cockpit, old girl."

At this, Dottie seemed more agitated and certainly puzzled as she watched the passing dinghy yet was hearing the voice coming from the radio in the cabin below.

As Drew approached the stern, Dottie followed, climbing through the *Owl*'s rigging and into the rear cockpit like a rabid chimpanzee, continually biting at the air. As she did, mucous slung from her nose and mouth, dripping down her chest and furthering the nightmare that had become of her jacket.

Circling the rear, around to the port side, Drew thought he may only have one shot at this. Dottie was certainly sick but also certainly focused and aware.

He spoke into the radio, much louder now, "Dotttiiiee!"

Dottie spun around and looked once more through the companionway for the source of the noise. Seeing nothing, she whipped back around as Drew throttled toward the *Owl*'s Bow.

Drew continued as he sped forward, yelling now, "Dottie, hey down here. Down here Dot, I'm down here."

Dottie was utterly disoriented, switching focus from the open companionway and the VHS below to the small boat that was approaching around to the bow again.

Drew readied the lasso by the time Dottie committed to

approach the bow at full steam and the bowsprit on the Island Packet made an easy target as the loop of line slid simply over both anchors. With a tug, it made hard purchase as Dottie came crashing into the pulpit. Bodily discharge from her rained down in ribbons on Drew as he throttled forward, line unspooling from the coil beneath his feet. 50 feet, life jacket, 50 feet reeled out behind him. Everything happening so fast, Drew almost let all the line run out before stopping to secure the end of the rope to the dinghy.

"Oh shit," he yelled, grabbing the line just before it went over the side. "Fuck, got to be smarter."

Once secure, the little dinghy's 6 hp dug in, but protested about the 37 foot behemoth it was attached to. At first, Drew doubted it could tow her, but once momentum set in, he was able to cross the distance of another 100 feet or so to *Hannah*, where he secured the tether.

Back aboard, Drew grabbed his sea anchor, rushed to *Hannah*'s bow, secured it to a cleat, and hurled the small orange parachute into the water.

Double checking the sea anchor's purchase, Drew turned and made his way back to *Hannah*'s cockpit-not taking his eyes off the boat in tow.

Dottie was still very agitated, yet curious now, about the life jacket that would sometimes suspend in midair when the lines pulled tight, but would then splash back down into the water, only to return airborne again.

Drew had been concerned that the weight of the ropes underwater, combined with the current, may pull the two boats together. That was certainly far from his objective. The life jacket was properly floating the towline in the middle and hopefully would serve its purpose well by keeping the vessels apart while *Hannah*'s sea anchor should keep the line tight.

Not knowing what to do next, he simply watched Dottie and waited for something, some change to occur, for this to somehow all go away. Dottie was a friend. Jack was a friend. Dottie was now having some kind of a breakdown and Jack was missing in action.

All Drew felt like he could do was simply drift.

Knowing attempts at sleep that night would be futile, Drew grabbed a wool blanket and lay out in the cockpit. Turning on the GPS he determined that he was safe enough offshore, there had not been any bad weather forecasts previously, and he was still drifting, gently south. As Dottie wished, they had begun their trip toward Savannah.

Staring at the *Owl of Athena*, Dottie was a heaving shadow on the bow as cabin lights were still illuminating the *Owl*'s port windows. They said, "Someone's home," but clearly, they were telling a lie.

Drew thought again about Jack. What had happened? It hadn't been twelve hours since this ordeal started and at that time everything had been fine. Thinking again about the dinghy dangling from their davits and the broken stanchions, Drew had to assume that Dottie must have gotten sick during the night and Jack had tried to escape her. He must have gone overboard possibly trying to swim to me, Drew thought. That could possibly explain the stanchions. Whatever happened, it had to have happened quickly. Jack would have been on the radio immediately, given the opportunity. If Jack had tried to swim to me but was injured in any way, the sharks – Drew thought to himself as he faded in and out of consciousness.

Dottie impatiently remained alert and focused on her prize in the distance.

Chapter 3

It wasn't the rising sun over the ocean the next morning that woke Drew so much as the tickle somewhere in the back of his brain reminding him that he was asleep on a boat, that was tied to another boat, that had a monster aboard.

Before he was even able to stretch his cramped legs, he was on his feet and began to recheck the work he had done the previous night, evaluating the security of the lines.

For Christ sakes, has Dottie been up the entire night, just staring at me? Drew thought, glancing across at the woman still swaying from side to side at the bow. Her ponytail had fallen free and her salt encrusted silver hair frizzed out, amplifying the disfigurement of her strained face. She paced back and forth, attention always dialed into Drew who disappeared into *Hannah*'s Cabin.

Below, it did not take long to survey his situation. He had prepared to meet the world head on.

- 100 gallons of fresh water combined between the holding tanks and the portable containers
- 30 days of freeze dried meals (the best cuisine REI and Wise produced)
- 15 cans of mixed vegetables
- 15 cans of Chef Boyardee Ravioli's (had since he was a kid)
- 15 cans of powdered soup
- 10 military MREs
- 1 AR-15 assault rifle (2 boxes of ammo)
- 1 Glock 19 semi-automatic pistol (100 rounds 9mm)
- 1 pistol grip Mossberg Marine Persuader (1 box of shells)
- AIS
- GPS
- Chartplotter
- Flare gun and flares
- Solar panels
- 400 amp hours of battery power

Rationing, I have two months, Drew figured, ripping open the foil of an MRE, grabbing a red bull out of his mini fridge, and heading back up to the cockpit.

Checking the fuel, he noticed that he had half a tank of diesel. He had planned to fill up with fuel and fresh produce before the actual voyage, but aside from that he was squared away.

Choking down the 370 calorie military issue brownie from the MRE, Drew grabbed his portable VHF and returned to his Dinghy. He didn't fuss with the dinghy's 6hp, but instead, relied on the tether between the two boats to make his investigative approach toward Dottie. She had now stopped her pacing and was leaning out at him from the *Owl*'s bow pulpit.

Drew was certain that Jack was not on the boat anymore and probably was not in any reasonable condition if he was. Drew was more interested to see if there was any part of Dottie still left aboard other than this croaking resemblance.

His answer came quickly.

20 Feet directly off the Owl's bow, Drew ceased forward motion. From Dottie's posture and Doberman-like glare, he was concerned she would attempt to try and take an airborne route to his tiny boat if he were to come any closer.

"Dottie, it's Andrew." Dottie had always called him by his full name as had his wife and he secretly appreciated it.

Louder this time, "Dottie, God dammit it's me!"

For a second, Dottie's expression seemed to go flat and confused but the rage washed it away just as quickly as it had come.

Drew's attempts were unavailing.

His eyes dropped to the teak railing that she and Jack so meticulously maintained. Dottie's steady flow of mucous and saliva was dripping onto it and drying as a crust as she lashed out again and again belting out that excruciating throat noise in response to Drew's presence.

"Crooooaaaat," she called out to him, "crooooooaaaaaaat."

I hate to see her like this. They are both lost, Drew thought, picturing Jack and Dottie walking up the dock smiling, Bella always running out ahead.

The sun had made its way high overhead and Drew lay back in *Hannah's* cockpit trying to relax with a flood of thoughts still pouring through his head. *Hannah's* boom was swinging back and forth gently, clanging the rigging like a dinner bell. "Come and get it," it called out across the water to Dottie.

Drew looked up at the sky and back to Dottie again. He had not seen another plane in the air since the military sortie had flown over the day before. There was still nothing coming across channel 16, either. Earlier, he thought he had seen what looked to be a shrimp boat off in the distance, but it was in the direction of the sun and he wasn't sure if his eyes were playing tricks on him.

This must have all happened quickly. How is this possible? This is the USA, this is 2014, we have guns, the military, and iPhones, and stuff like this GPS, that shows me right where I am.

At that, he flipped on the Garmin. Still giving a position, he knew that the satellites were still operational.

Drew wondered. So how am I not sick? After all, they were my slip mates. We breathed pretty much the same air and shopped at the same stores. Hell, I was all over their boat before they left. What am I missing?

Staring back at Dottie, he believed that she was indeed sick and was probably not going to recover. She also certainly meant to do him harm if given the opportunity–but why? Rabies? Was she contagious? Shit, she had even slung bloody snot onto him and yet he wasn't on his bow screeching and making a fuss. Jack, of course, was not there to tell his side of things, so what next?

With the ocean gently lapping against the side of Hannah's hull and the gentle rocking motion, Drew closed his eyes. The broken stanchions could be heard hitting against the *Owl of Athena*'s hull. Tock, tock, tock, ticking time, a metronome.

Time passed and night fell.

Chapter 4

It was the sound of approaching twin Cummins 370B diesels that brought Drew to consciousness again. The 44 foot Huckin's Ortega was on him fast and its wake nearly knocked Drew off the cockpit bench before he could get to his feet. The boat was making a wide loop around their flotilla and Drew could see the backlit *Minerva* on the yacht's transom.

Drew grabbed his air horn from a cockpit pouch and leapt onto *Hannah*'s deck as the captain aboard the *Minerva* was spotlighting the woman on the bow of the *Owl of Athena*.

Drew blew the horn and motioned him over.
The captain responded by motoring forward but kept his distance, just enough to shout over the now idling diesels.

Drew could see that the guy was handsome, in his early thirties, well built, and wearing a wet suit peeled down to his waste.

"What the fuck, crazy 'life of pie' shit is this?" he called out, anxiously staring down from the fly bridge, first blinding Drew with the spotlight, then beaming it out along the tether toward Dottie again.

"We had an accident here," Drew said.

"The whole world had an accident bro, and from the looks of it, you just got an appetizer portion."

Drew noticed this guy was jumpy. The beam of the spotlight was dancing in his shaky hand.

The man climbed down onto the spacious rear deck of the *Minerva* and over to her starboard rail for a closer look at Drew. On the man's descent, Drew noticed a handgun tucked into the wetsuit at the small of his back. Now face to face, Drew could see white powder around the guy's nose. Jumpy indeed.

It made Drew anxious.

"What happened, what's going on?" Drew asked.

The guy eased a bit. He probably had confirmed now that Drew had not come down with this affliction. "I probably don't know much more than you. I was diving this boat, replacing the prop zincs for this rich prick when the shit hit the fan, at least at the marina. I heard people screaming and as soon as I had my head out of the water, I saw them," he said.

He shined the beam back over at Dottie who was panting hungrily and dazed by the light. "They were running free, lots of them. People I knew. They were attacking other people. The only thing I could do was reach up and cut the lines securing the boat. The current took me out of the berth. Once free, I climbed aboard and found the keys were in the ignition," he said, pulling in the severed dock lines he had been towing. "I just tried to get away as fast as I could. I caught a bit of the news on the satellite entertainment center before it shut off. They said something about the water. They mentioned it was happening coast to coast at random locations across the country. An 'epidemic' they were calling it." He paused, "People call me 'Shark' by the way."

"I'm Drew."

"Look, it's been nice to meet you Drew, but I need to roll

out of here," Shark said, making his ascent back up to the fly bridge. "I've got almost enough fuel to get me to the Bahamas and I would have taken yours but you need it as much as I do-and I don't steal." He chuckled, gave a quick salute, and patted the wheel of the *Minerva* gingerly. Putting her in gear he called out, "If you have a weapon, go ahead and shoot that bitch, I don't want to waste any of my bullets-and be careful, that is only Stage-1. When they become Stage-2s you have to shoot them in the head. That's what Fox news said."

With that, the *Minerva* was gone.

Drew slumped back on the cockpit bench. He had prepared himself for the loneliness he was going to face on his circumnavigation attempt but that plan had changed and a new, unexpected wave of despair washed over him. For the first time in a long time he wanted to cry but nothing came, as he had already cried all of his tears for his wife and son. He was running on empty.

Drew looked over at Dottie again.

"Ok," he said to himself, disappearing into the cabin and returning to the cockpit with his rifle.

Drew turned on the green light laser of his ar-15 and targeted Dottie, who was still crouching at the bow pulpit like a madwoman with a walker.

Respectfully, Drew aimed at center mass and fired two rounds. Dottie stood and then faltered back, crashing against the mast. Drew could see her silhouette in the moonlight as she lay slumped against it. She was dead. Devastated, Drew lowered the weapon.

Lying back on the cockpit bench, Drew contemplated what he had just done and thought about turning the weapon on himself. It was a liberating idea that lingered with him as his thoughts drifted. It should have been me…

"Drew you fucking debutante, you killed my wife and now we are going to have a little chat."

Jack had now replaced his wife on the bow of the Owl of Athena and was gnashing his teeth with the same fervor. In his hands was the tether between the boats. Jack was hauling in the umbilical as it coiled at his feet. He was in his bright yellow Grunden's offshore jacket with his hood tied tightly; the strained muscles in his face twisted his features into almost unrecognizable contortions.

"You killed my Dottie," Jack said again, hauling in the life jacket, 25 feet and closing.

"Drew!" Jack squawked again, eyes burning and teeth cracking together, "This is all your fault!"

Drew slammed awake, drenched in sweat–despite the cooling ocean air. The moon was sinking in the distance, clearing room for the sun. The *Owl of Athena* was back to the full length of her tether and Jack was not there.

Neither was Dottie.

Drew got to his feet.

Am I going insane? Is it me that is sick? He reached out and grabbed at the solar panel trying to steady himself. Touching the cool flat surface of its aluminum frame was like a pinch to let him know that this was all real.

Still in confusion, he reached under the cockpit seat,

grabbed his flare gun, and sent a Para-flare out above the *Owl of Athena.*

In the torch lit sky, Drew could see that Dottie was still aboard and very much animated.

I killed her, he thought.

Dottie was now in the cockpit of the *Owl* and appeared to be moving, but with slower mechanics. Her hair had apparently gotten caught in the bimini top framework and she was struggling against it. Oblivious to her entrapment, arms held out before her, she clawed at the air, trying blindly to make purchase on something.

Her gaze turned up to the drifting flare. She seemed momentarily disinterested in Drew.

"Dottie," Drew called out to her.

Her attention was immediately captured by his voice. It had turned on a switch somewhere inside her head that caused her to focus back on him. She was hungry, clearly, but there was lethargy to her movements that had not been there before. This must be Stage-2, he thought, but I killed her. He could clearly see the exit wounds drying as deep maroon splotches on the back of her jacket.

The flare winked out as it met the ocean and with that Dottie's attention on Drew evaporated.

The sun began to rise, continuing to do its job even in this new world and it seemed to say, "Don't mind me mate, I can see you have your hands full." Even so, its light was a welcome sight and it was three fingers in the sky by the time Drew was back in the Dinghy.

"Groundhogs day," he muttered, checking his rifle and firing up the sputtering outboard.

Dottie had noticed him again and was straining forward against her bindings. Her hair was pulled tight, stretching her face, giving her the countenance of a lizard. Previously gentle eyes were now bulging orbs.

"Jesus Christ," Drew said, reaching the *Owl* end of the tether and approached the cockpit to starboard.

Dottie wasn't glaring at him intently with the sense of awareness she had before. She stared through him, her teeth snapping together. She seemed to be trying to speak but only raspy, hissing moans came out–the sounds alligators make. She was hungry and clearly after him.

Drew raised the rifle and did as Fox news had instructed. One shot to the head and Dottie disgracefully hung from the bimini framework by her hair like a troll doll on the rearview of a 64 Impala.

"I'm so sorry Dottie," Drew said, and tears actually came this time. The loneliness and regret washed over him like tidal sets. Now he felt truly alone.

"So what you got for me next?" Drew cursed and stared at the sky, angry at a God he didn't have faith in.

Drew floated, suspended in time, holding onto the dangling stanchion of the *Owl of Athena* before he decided to board her. There were risks involved here. What was this? How was it spread? It is contagious now? Regardless, something aboard this boat clearly must have caused this and he needed to find out what.

He climbed aboard, steering clear of Dottie's lifeless body as he first walked the deck. Crossing around to port, things were ok. At the bow, Dottie's spew was drying on the pulpit as was the blood spatter from the rifle rounds meeting their target. Around to starboard, Drew could now see signs of struggle at the broken stanchions. Clearly, Jack had been hanging on at one point, out of reach of his attacker–but also out of earshot of the *Hannah Cole.*

Drew glanced over at Dottie whose sea glass eyes stared off in either direction. This must have happened fast, he thought, not even time to radio me.

In the cockpit, Drew crouched at the companionway and peered into the *Owl of Athena*'s main salon. The well oiled teak and mahogany interior was relatively unmolested despite everything being covered in Dottie's juices. The leather cushioned settee at starboard had plates laid out. In the galley, vegetables were already turning brown on the cutting board. Flies were buzzing around the gimbaled stove that gently rocked an uneaten pot of stew that had long gone room temp. The only thing out of place was Dottie's favorite mug she had purchased from a Starbucks in Puerto Rico and it lay broken on the floor.

Drew remembered what the Shark guy had said about the water and pictured Jack walking up to him as he leveled his holding tanks back at the marina. Approaching in his touristy Hawaiian shirt and Maui Jim sunglasses, he said, "What are you, some kind of a debutante? Filling your holding tanks with bottled water? I'm surprised your hailing port isn't San Francisco."

"I know, I know Jack, I was just waiting for you to say something. I do it to keep the scale from building up in these old tanks," Drew responded, rolling his eyes.

"Sure you do. You're always fussing with this thing and

not taking her sailing. You're the D dock debutante," he declared, waving dismissively.

They had enjoyed jabs at each other ever since. Jack was an older guy and life had made him a bit rough around the edges but he was good hearted. He certainly had his own way of doing things and that was just the way you did it. Filling up the freshwater holding tank with the hose was just what you did, and drinking from the galley tap was ok, because that, my friends, is what old sailors do.

Drew descended into the small but comfortable space. He looked around. Certainly, if communications had gone down so fast, those infected must have been able to spread it to others. Was it terrorism? The fucking Muslims? God help the United State and possibly the rest of the world, he thought as he approached the V-Birth, steering clear of the human discharge that Dottie had left behind.

Leaning in, he glanced around at Dottie's things. This had been her space, an agreement she made with Jack.

Muffled noises came from the rear cabin.

Drew froze. An image of his dream the night before flashed to mind-Jack.

Drew's stomach clenched and he felt like vomiting.

He swung around.

"Thump."

The noise came again from behind the closed aft cabin door. Next to the companionway steps, it was right beside the only immediate exit.

"Thump, Thump."

Hearing the sound once more, Drew dove toward the companionway and scrambled up into the cockpit.

Then he heard the bark.

Bella's yip exploded the silence in the cabin and made Drew feel as if his heart was going to explode. Pausing in the companionway to catch his breath, Drew waited for his state to shift gears from pure terror to mild fear. Heart still racing, he dropped back into the salon and opened the Bronze plaqued door that read "CREW."

A bright orange flash ran out between Drew's legs. It was Bella, sporting her "Ruffwear" life jacket-the one with the handle on the back. Certainly dehydrated, she was no worse for wear.

Drew squatted down and Bella jumped into his arms, licking his face, full body wag.

"I am happy to see you too girl, more than you know."

Drew grabbed a sealed Pisani from the mini fridge and poured it into a dish for Bella. While preparing her a bowl of food, she drank heartily, pausing between gulps to look-up at him with certain canine gratitude. Drew looked toward Bella's cabin. She had probably been spooked by whatever was going on outside the door and had maintained silence until she heard him.

"Smart girl," Drew said, rubbing the tiny head.

The little Gremlin, as Drew called her, watched patiently as he rummaged through galley drawers in search of what he needed. Grabbing a pair of scissors he exited the cockpit and cut Dottie's hair free from its entanglement. Getting her limp body down through the companionway and to the v-birth was a bit of a challenge but he managed after several attempts.

Finding Dottie a fresh jacket and wiping her face clear, Drew shut the door to the v-berth.

"You and Jack will be missed old girl."

In a settee hatch, Drew found Jack's colt 1911 .45 he was issued in Vietnam as a green beret. Still in its hip holster with belt, he strapped it on.

Drew made several trips back and forth carrying provisions over to the *Hannah Cole* and Bella took every trip, staying close to Drew and never letting him out of her sight. He was able to attain more canned food, tools, .45 rounds, dog food (just a single five pound bag-looks like people food for you Bella), batteries, candles, flash lights, two canisters of propane, flares, first aid kits, Jack's overboard bag, and miscellaneous other items. More importantly, Jack had strapped 4 jerry cans of diesel up near the mast and Drew had been able to transfer fuel from the *Owl of Athena*'s tanks to his own. That put his estimated range on motor alone to 300 nautical miles.

It was getting late in the afternoon and *Hannah* was clearly sitting much lower in the water with all the added weight. Drew made one last trip back to the Owl of Athena, alone.

Out of respect for his fallen companions, he walked around deck, tidying up ropes, cheesing the lines, and then he went below to straighten up the interior (shipshape as Jack would have liked it).

With a final look around, he opened the door under the galley sink and cut the hose running up to the basin and seawater poured out from it. He was in his dinghy cutting the umbilical between the boats by the time the *Owl of Athena's* bilge pumps first kicked on.

The sun was setting and the sky had turned pink and turquoise by the time the *Owl* was making her last struggles. With Bella in his lap, Drew looked on as the beautiful boat foundered and then gradually slipped below the surface.

The plan had changed. Everything had changed.

Chapter 5

"Bella, we have important work to do," Drew said in a matter-of-fact tone, picking her up by the handle on the little life jacket and carrying her down through *Hannah*'s companionway. He sighed when he looked around at the massive clutter of supplies and felt like an easy candidate to be visited by Matt Paxton, the extreme cleaning specialist from that reality show, "Hoarder's".

In the midst of the clutter, he sat at his circular settee table with Bella and began unrolling charts.

If anything was certain, it wasn't the weather and not having communications made things difficult. He had radar but needed the long term forecast. When their party had left the marina, the forecast was to be as it had been for the last couple of days. This could always change for the worse and finding a harboring gunk hole was probably his best course of action.

He booted his laptop and interfaced with the onboard navigation system. Thank god for satellites. His position, Latitude 3211.2357' N, Longitude 07928.7166 W, put him approximately 80 miles off the southern coast of South Carolina. What to do? What to do? Getting close to shore meant unknown risks, but it also promised a possible cell phone connection. Either way, it meant more information than he had and he couldn't just stay drifting in the Atlantic indefinitely.

He closed the laptop.

Drew decided that he and Bella would straighten up in the morning and set sail. The destination was to be Beaufort, South Carolina and the primary objective was to get within cell phone range.

Drew went out on deck to check rigging before retiring. In the distance he could see several lights on the eastern horizon—other boats. Interesting the radio silence, he thought to himself. Channel 16 had been on the entire time.

He wondered about the people aboard those ships, what they knew? What was their plan? Silent, like me, clearly. Are they silent for safety? Or were they perhaps silent because they had changed as Dottie had, out there, in this vacuum, with stars shining brightly across the dome of the sky, moving as they had for years.

Jack did not return to his dreams that night. The *Owl* was now gone and the tether was broken forever.

✥ ✥ ✥

Drew was in their small two story house on Bull Street, preparing lunch and looking out the kitchen window to the front yard. Hannah was chasing Cole with a garden hose around the cheap blue baby pool they had purchased at the K-mart in West Ashley. Drew was cutting the crust off Cole's pb and j when Hannah dropped the hose and looked off in a direction that was blocked from Drew's view. She seemed to flinch, then put her hand to her mouth. Grabbing Cole up, she stumbled, nearly losing balance as her shin caught the edge of the plastic pool. Drew dropped the knife on the tile countertop and bolted to the front door to meet his wife. He was almost there when Hannah came crashing through, Cole under her arm, flapping like a Raggedy Andy doll. He began to cry. Hannah slammed the solid front door and slid over the heavy ancient bolts that secured it shut.

"Get upstairs Drew," she screamed. She was frantic. Drew knew what was coming with the first thud that hit the front door. Hannah screamed again as they bolted up the stairs. Cole was wailing.

The first floor of the house had a long living room with sliding glass doors at the far end. The kitchen was at the other end and there was a staircase in the middle leading up to a loft that overlooked the living room. The foyer at the top of the stairs led to two bedrooms and a bathroom via a small hallway. After reaching the loft, Drew hurled a Brown Pottery Barn couch and two loveseats over the railing onto the staircase below.

"Get into Cole's Bedroom," Drew commanded.

The sliding glass door shattered. Drew heaved his wife's massive mahogany sideboard down the staircase where it smashed into the growing pile of furniture from the loft. Two Stage-1s were in the living room now. One was a man in a Charleston City Police uniform with a balding crew-cut and the other, a middle aged nurse in blood-soaked scrubs. A MUSC *badge identified her as Amanda Matthews. They tore through the downstairs slinging mucus and human ooze all over his wife's untouchables. Blinded by rage, they finally noticed Drew as the 55 inch family Samsung smashed down on top of the pile below. Looking down again, the police man was gone, it was Drew's father, then it was his mother, then his college roommate. The faces on the monsters were changing. More entered the room from the demolished rear door, his high school chemistry teacher, Mr Parks, his drill instructor from basic training, an old girlfriend, all possessed with the fury. More faces now, changing. Emergency vehicle sirens were blaring off in the distance. Drew passed through the small hallway into Cole's room joining his wife and son. He slammed the door shut and slid Cole's dresser in front of it.*

"Get out on the roof, now!" He screamed.

On the rooftop the trio witnessed the carnage erupting down the street, fast and ferocious, like lions on Christians.

The window exploded behind them.

Drew opened his eyes to a light rain misting across the top of the v-birth hatch. Bella was curled up tightly beside his head, warming his neck.

It was morning and Mary Kitchen corned beef hash straight from the can seemed to get the mental juices flowing again. He wasn't feeling hungry, not feeling well at all actually, and it was difficult to choke down-but he knew he needed the energy for the trip back to the mainland. Spooning in another mouthful of the greasy pink mash, he updated his pilots log on the previous few days events and finished by recording:

Setting course for Parris Island, South Carolina to establish possible military contact. Choosing to diesel the entire leg. Don't want to waste the fuel but needed to make land on time and having canvas up may draw possible unwanted attention. From current location, estimated time of arrival: 1:00 AM Tuesday, November 18.

Drew bent down and let Bella lick the remainder of the hash from the spoon.

"Time to weigh anchor, girl."

It had been grey most of the morning. The rain had cleared up but the air was heavy and barometer was still falling. Bella rounded up the courage to venture out on deck and inspect her new vessel, first mate duties, while the diesel pushed *Hannah* along nicely at 6 knots.

Fear of the unknown and what he was possibly headed for kept Drew's mind from the dropping temperature. He was nearly shivering when he spotted an out of season shrimp boat ahead, recognizable by the telltale V made by the net booms.

Debating on changing course to avoid contact, Drew tried the handheld VHF.

Channel 16: "Commercial fishing vessel, this is the *Sailing vessel Hannah Cole*, heading to your starboard."

No response.

Again, "Commercial fishing vessel, this is the *Hannah Cole,* approaching you to starboard. Do you copy? Over."

Silence.

Drew maintained course, noticing again the weight of the .45 strapped to his waist and feeling comforted by it. Within half an hour, he was in range to hear the seagulls that swarmed around the rust streaked hull of the fishing boat. Lifting his binoculars, he could make out a fading name on the bow.

"Fishing vessel *Lazarus*, this is the *Hannah Cole* approaching your starboard, do you copy?"

Silence.

"*Lazarus*, this is the..." Drew began, but then spotted three figures aboard who were now clearly visible in their bright yellow coveralls.

Fumbling in the cockpit bag, he withdrew an air horn. His three short blasts pierced the air.

Bella seemed agitated and was out on the bow now.

"Bella, get back here!"

She ignored him, fixed on the boat they were approaching.

Drew lifted the binoculars again. There had been no response from the horn blasts, but it appeared that the individuals in the yellow suits were waiving their arms as if attempting to hail him. Within minutes, Drew did not need the binoculars to see that those aboard were not trying to hail him. The vessel was clearly not under power and her nets hung slack in the water. Seagulls lined the gunnels and took roost on the beams. Those in the air flitted about, screeching with excitement as the more courageous ones dive bombed the yellow figures that comically tried to bat away their squawking aggressors.

A large one took purchase on the head of one of the sailors. He ineffectively flailed his arms to unseat the unwanted nag that was apparently pecking at his scalp. A couple quick jerks and it took to the air with something in its beak.

Drew closed the gap to 50 yards and slowed *Hannah* to

a crawl. He could hear Bella's growl over the muted diesel; she remained at the bow, hackle up and focused on what lay ahead. Drew understood that whatever had taken place aboard the *Owl of Athena* had clearly taken place aboard the *Lazarus*.

Three more short blasts on the air horn and he had the attention of those aboard. Drew closed to 25 yards and began to circle around *Lazarus*'s stern to Starboard.

At this distance, he could now make out a fourth individual in the pilot house, perhaps the captain, an older man in a black turtleneck. He had taken notice of the passing sailboat and spider webbed the near bulletproof glass with his snarling face. The window blossomed with blood splatter as the maniac smashed against it repeatedly.

Drew's attention snapped back to the three individuals on the stern. Two were clearly dead and reanimated. One man, Drew could see, had lost most of his face to the incessant birds pulling at his drooping flesh. The whiteness of his cheekbones stood out through the red carnage of his face.

The second man had feathers and blood matting his disaster of a beard. He had obviously taken hold of one of the flying tormentors and made a meal of it. Appearing as if he had been mauled by a wild animal, his intestines strung out from the black gore hole torn into his belly. As the man batted at the nipping seagulls, Drew could see that three fingers on his right hand appeared to be bitten off.

The third man was raging out with the same enthusiasm as the man in the pilot house, rabid as Dottie had been during her first phase of whatever this sickness was. Focused and clearly alive, he was younger, probably handsome at one time. He crouched at the gunnel in his bloodstained coveralls, panting heavily as this new visitor passed to starboard.

Just then, as the wind shifted briefly, it was the smell of fish rotting in the sun, seagull shit, and the potent, coppery, mineral smell of blood wafting in the breeze that caused Drew's stomach to tighten and he lost his Mary Kitchen corned beef breakfast over *Hannah*'s side.

Drew wiped his mouth, looked and noticed Bella. With steady growl through bared teeth, she was on full alert.

Suddenly, as if in retaliation for the fallen companion, a large seagull smashed into the bearded man's face, tugged out an eyeball, and gulped it down in two hard swallows as it took to the air.

Alfred Hitchcock flashed to mind and Drew threw up again.

Regaining composure, he came around the fishing boat twice more and the *Lazarus* crew moved with him as he circled; now less intent on the pestering birds, they concentrated on Drew. The croaks of the live one barked out across the water and made him feel like he would pass out at any moment.

As he motored by, it was curious that they did not attack each other. There had been a struggle, but once now infected, they appeared almost neutral to each other's existence.

The Stage-1 suddenly lost interest in Drew-maybe giving up to the gap that separated them. It disappeared behind two crab pots and dragged out the body of a fifth sailor that had been previously hidden from view.

Like a hyena, it dug into the soft belly of its fallen shipmate, bit loose a yellow mass of belly fat, and swallowed it down. It flashed wild eyes between Drew and its kill as it came up's between bites.

Drew didn't need to see anymore and straightened the tiller to his original course as *Hannah* made her final pass.

The skies overhead were heavy and darkening and Drew wanted to make good time to Port Royal Sound. Throttling forward, he played the events that had just unfolded over and over in his mind. \

Five men aboard: two Stage-1s, two Stage-2s, one man dead and being eaten. Waves of terror and confusion swept over Drew at the thought-one was being eaten. Jesus.

The two Stage-1s, the one in the cabin and the one on deck, had possibly been the ones that drank "the Kool-Aid" and must have attacked their shipmates. Those not turned were probably able to trap the Stage-1 in the pilot house-but they must have succumbed to injuries caused by the one that had been eating his crewmate. Jesus. It was a puzzle and he felt too frazzled trying to put the pieces together.

He motored on as a light drizzle set in.

Chapter 6

By 11:30 PM there was a steady rain, the wind had shifted, and with it brought a putrid smoke that hung low over the ocean. It reminded Drew of the smell at a drag strip: burning tires, metallic brake and clutch, and barbequed meat. Combined with the rain, the smoke was causing miserable visibility as he passed the first channel markers at the entrance to Port Royal sound.

Drew checked his iPhone.

Still, no signal.

He tried texting his friend Stephen Meese but it only came back as undelivered and his Google Maps app was not seeing him on GPS.

Drew checked his chart plotter and verified marine traffic on the AIS. Three AIS targets were coming up. One was a tugboat currently located on Skull Creek. There was also a 65 foot motor yacht and from the looks of its position and depth, it appeared to be beached on Hilton Head, not visible, but off Drew's port beam. The third was a 100 foot yacht sitting apparently moored at Skull Creek Marina on Hilton Head Island.

Drew steamed along at a safe four knots and followed

course up to the red and green channel markers at the entrance to the Beaufort River. That's when he began to see the bodies in the water.

Bella began barking at what appeared to be a floating block of foam just off the bow. As the object came abeam, Drew saw that it wasn't much more than a torso in a life jacket. He put a light on it. The head arms and legs were missing, chewed away. He noticed the United States Marine corps BDU blouse it still wore was in tatters as it drifted by.

He got explanation for the missing extremities of the Marine as he passed a second body, this one a golfer. Small hammerheads splashed and agitated the water around it as they stripped the flesh from its arms. Coming into closer view, the checked herringbone pants the corpse was still wearing stood out against the black sea.

25 yards away, he pulled alongside a drifting inflatable dinghy, slathered with bloodstains. There was no occupant.

Ahead to port, the light from the Parris Island training compound was revealed through the thickening, greasy air. Parris Island was the quiet. There were no planes, vehicles, sirens, alarms, or screams-just sound of the breeze through the rigging and the puttering of *Hannah*'s diesel. The rain began to let off, clarifying an orange glow that was lighting the sky like distant fireworks through the smoke. The breeze brought heat off the bow and was warming the chilly air. Just ahead of him, it appeared that the entire island of Port Royal was on fire.

Drew tucked Hannah in close to Parris Island, depth permitting. There was waterfront housing along the coast, probably for officers, he thought. He could not make out the houses but for dim flecks of light through the smoke. The wind was shifting again, allowing for better visibility but it wasn't any relief from the smell. His head was pounding.

As the lights of the island's military training facility came into focus, Drew passed by a well-lit grassy field backed by a large building and another tall structure he couldn't make out. His Chartplotter street map view showed the building to be "the Lyceum."

It wasn't the uniformed figures lumbering around in the field in front that caught Drew's eye, but the lit flagpole in the middle. Through the smoke, and in a pink haze from the burning island to the west, the American flag could be seen at half mast, flying inverted.

The sight of it suddenly made Drew feel naked and exposed. His eyes dropped to the marines in the field, a mixture of uniform types, actually out of place for the surroundings, they took no notice of the passing vessel. It was clear that the factory that produced some of the toughest American badasses was now closed for business. The force field we all feel as Americans was down–the security blanket had been jerked away in an instant.

Not venturing closer, Drew changed to a northwest course into Cowen Creek and put Cat Island to port. Away from the generator lit Parris Island, Drew chose instead to head into the darkness.

It was nearly midnight and Drew felt rudderless, confused and exhausted. His head was still throbbing from the acrid smell, blurring clear thought, as he leaned in, scanning the onboard Garmin GPS maps and the SEAiq app on his iPhone.

Bella leaned in too, as if to ponder with Drew the decision on where to go next.

Cat Island, South Carolina, Drew scanned his guidebook, "Despite it's far-away-feel and protected environment, Cat Island is one of the closest communities to downtown Beaufort. The community offers amazing amenities such as golf, tennis courts, 5 pools, a British pub and a boat landing. The Island is home to the Sanctuary Golf Club, a par-71 course designed by George W Cobb. The community has full-service restaurant with great food and atmosphere. Live oak trees, beautiful wetlands, and other natural resources attracted the development of Cat Island's more upscale, newer, and most expensive homes, many of which offering deep water access and navigable waterways with quick ocean access."

"Sounds like a safe bet, Bella. Maybe if we settle in soon we can still be up in time for 9 holes in the morning," Drew said, trying to elevate his mood with sarcasm.

Bella stretched paws forward with her tail in the air, held it for a second, then shook it off as if in agreement.

Cat Island was dark, very dark, but out of direct line from the smoke. Visibility was improved but he still had the blackness to deal with. To his port, solar lights gave away the position of the long piers that jutted out to deep water. These were the only markers of the expensive homes that lay hidden in the shadows of the tree line. Drew reviewed the GPS again and made his way to one pier in particular. It belonged to a house out on a small peninsula that was surrounded by wetlands and at the end of a cul-de-sac as far as he could tell electronically.

He set course for a row of tiny solar lights marking its position and went for a pass.

From the looks of it, he had dealt himself a good hand, all things considered. It was an L shaped pier that had a floating dock at the end. Birthed inside the L was a 36 foot Pursuit fishing boat. Moored alongside the pier next to it was a platform barge that had been putting in an expansion and had already put two outer pilings in place.

The portholes were dark on the Pursuit, *Class Action* and she looked vacant. The immediate advantage Drew could see was that if he parked at the outer side of the pier, the *Class Action* would perhaps at least partially block him from view of the house.

With that, he backed off the diesel and brought *Hannah* into neutral. She slowed and nudged against one of the new, outer pilings.

Instantly, on his feet and moving, Bella hopping from the cockpit to the deck in pursuit, he tied off. Using the piling to pivot, Drew took advantage of the current to swing his stern around, closing the gap to the floating dock. As she came around, Drew tossed a line and caught a cleat, securing *Hannah* in such a way that she was somewhat nose out. Cutting the line would allow him to quickly swing away from the dock in either direction depending on the current if there were to be an issue here. As he was now situated, he arranged about a 4 foot gap from the stern down to the lower floating dock. It was an easy hop down and a running jump to get back on and it seemed that Bella wouldn't be tempted to hop off and explore. He could have opted to moor off, but he felt like that might make him a target—especially when daylight came. He assumed he would not want to be out in the open. In addition, the thought of dragging anchor or debris damage led to his decision.

Drew stared again at the dark tree line. He was exhausted, hadn't had time to process anything yet, and he was starving but knew he didn't have the luxury of having the night off as he needed to survey his position.

He peeled the foil from a MRE and swallowed the beef stew without tasting it. Unwrapping a Wise Cheesy Lasagna for Bella, he stared up the pier and back down at the floating dock as if it were electrified.

So who was Mr. Class Action? Now it was a game of playing the demographic. He could either be a fat and friendly old southern lawyer looking like Kernel Sanders–ready to offer him a handshake and an Amstel light–or he could be a full blown Stage-1, ready to eat the pink center from his middle like the sailor on the shrimp boat. His nerves were ramping up as he contemplated all of the options in-between. Any way you looked at it, he was officially trespassing now and there was a good chance the owner of the *Class Action* both fished-and hunted. Drew's only advantage would be the *Hannah Cole*. A fellow boat owner may see a cruising sailboat manned by a single captain and a Chihuahua as fairly inert. He could only hope.

"Baby steps," he said to himself as his Sperry's made first contact with the floating dock. At first, it felt good to feel somewhat solid ground beneath his feet, but a sudden paranoia quickly melted that away. Suddenly, the windows of the fishing boat felt too dark and the pier seemed too short, closer to the pitch blackness.

His heart raced as he took a step toward the *Class Action* just as Bella yipped from the cockpit of the *Hannah Cole*, demanding assistance across the void.

"Jesus Bella, you scared the fuck out of me, again. Quiet down."

Bella yipped again.

"Bella, stay," Drew demanded, trying to keep it to a whisper.

She yipped again in defiance.

Giving up, Drew reached out and Bella leapt the gap into his arms.

"Ok girl, you pain in my ass," he said, setting her down.

Drew noticed she wasn't taking interest in the quiet *Class Action* and that eased his mind. He pulled the .45 from his side holster and stepped aboard.

The companionway door was black tinted Lexan and Drew couldn't see inside. It was comforting to see it was padlocked from the outside. Drew thumbed back the trigger as he wrapped the barrel of the Colt against it.

No response, empty.

Drew looked up and saw that Bella had already run half way down the pier but seemed to be keeping Drew within her sights. That was a good sign. He probably should have had her on a leash, but he wasn't thinking straight. Last thing he needed was for a damn Chihuahua to bring any attention. She was waiting for him though, keeping cool as a cucumber.

He surveyed the surroundings again. Looking down the coast, he could see neighboring docks, some with boats, some not. Solar powered led lights marked their existence. The pier he was on was about 6 feet wide with a waist high railing on either side. Peering over, he decided if he had to, the best course of action would be to hop over and into the water at any sign of trouble. He could always swim to a neighboring dock if need be. So far there had been no disturbance caused by his arrival and he wanted to keep it that way.

Drew winced at every hollow board creak of the weathered planks as Bella led their way down the pier toward the main property. She was sniffing around ahead of him and still didn't seem to be alarmed. This eased Drew's mind from the tendrils of Spanish moss that seemed to dance among the low branches of the overhanging live oaks in the distance.

The pier opened out onto a large deck that made up the lower of two tiers. There was a small flight of stairs that led to an upper tiled deck and finally to a Frank Lloyd Wright styled house with an infinity pool. Drew could see the house itself appeared to be a sprawling one story made entirely of large panes of glass broken up only by large French doors and some subtle framework. The house was situated on a peninsula and offered excellent views of both the canal and the marsh preserve from its windows.

He was anxious, every heartbeat was a kick to the chest, and his knuckles were white around the handle of the 1911 as he made his way up to the pool deck level and around the backside of the house to a porch at the rear.

Drew cupped his hands around his eyes and peered into the dark living room. It appeared to be vacant.

Grabbing the handle of the sliding door, he checked, and it slid open, gently in its track.

Bella darted in.

"Bella, wait," Drew whispered in frustration, but she disappeared into the shadows of the home, ignoring his request.

Senses on high alert, Drew stepped in after her and scrutinized the surroundings.

He clicked on a small battery operated penlight.

It was an expansive space with high ceilings, hardwood

floors, and white leather furniture. A large stone fireplace was off to the right. The mantle was adorned with family photographs and a large glass sculpture. To the left, the space transitioned into a slate grey professional kitchen with a massive bar for entertaining. Mr. Class Action had done well for himself.

Comforted by lack of report from Bella, Drew called out, "anyone home?"

At first, the only response he got were Bella's toenails clicking on the hardwood floor as she passed from room to room, investigating the area.

That is when he heard the music, Neil Young, "…somewhere on a desert highway, she rides a Harley Davidson…" It was distant and muffled.

Drew froze in panic and felt his legs go shaky. He felt like he was going to collapse right there on the white shag area rug.

There was a slight rumble felt inside the house he was only noticing now.

It was a car, a running car.

"Oh, god" Drew muttered to himself. Again, he called out louder this time, "Hello, anyone home?" He thought of Adam the Woo–creator of adamthewoo.com–an internet vlogger that he followed before the world moved on. Adam would post videos of his urban exploration adventures online. These videos would often show Adam calling out the same thing before trespassing into the unknown.

Drew took a step forward, Bella at his heels, looking up at him. Passing around the stone fireplace to the right, he began down a small hallway and could smell gasoline, fumes, and exhaust. A closed door marked the entrance to what appeared to be the garage. Pausing outside of it, the music was louder now.

He expected someone to burst through the door at any second and either tear him apart or blow his head off.

Drew raised the 1911 and pointed it at the door.

"Hello? Anyone home?" he called.

The fumes were noxious in the hallway and were burning his nostrils. Grabbing the door handle, he turned it and swung the door forward into the three car garage lit by the dim pink glow of driving lights.

Through a fog of exhaust fumes he made out the shape of a silver classic corvette stingray convertible with its top down. A man in a suit was slumped over in the driver's seat, clearly dead.

Drew moved forward to the vehicle, keeping his eyes on the driver. It was an older man in his early 60s, Mr. Class Action maybe? His face was grey and he had the signs of carbon monoxide poisoning. Drew nudged the side of the man's head with the barrel of the 1911.

The man didn't move.

Slowly, reaching across him with trembling hands, he shut off the cars engine and took the keys out of the ignition, silencing Neil's harmonica.

After taking his first true breath since entering the garage, he erupted into a fit of coughing. He returned to the living room, to a large foyer, and over to a large mahogany and glass front door. Peering through the panes he could see a front entrance with a circular drive that converged down a driveway that disappeared into the hanging smoke from the fires. The wind must be shifting again, Drew thought. He felt like he was being swallowed.

Bella escorted Drew as he scoped out the rest of the house. There was a luxuriously decorated large master bedroom with a marble spa bath off of the living room and two smaller guest rooms and a bath down a hallway off of the kitchen.

Nobody else was in the house.

Drew returned to the kitchen and opened the massive double doors of the Sub-zero fridge.

Not an Amstel light, but even better, Drew thought, grabbing a surprisingly cold bottled Pepsi out of the fridge. He swallowed it down in two big pulls.

Setting the empty bottle on the granite counter, he noticed a nearly empty bottle of Oban single malt scotch and a note.

It read, "Burt, out to hot yoga and the grocery, should be back by 7:30. Text if you need me to pick anything up while I'm out. Heart, Millie.

Drew flicked the knob on the white enamel stove. A blue flame came to life, gas. Drew glanced over at the brick fire place and saw the pilot light he hadn't noticed before. Maybe I can take a hot shower. That will have to wait for tomorrow he thought, grabbing another Pepsi and returning to the front door.

There was a cul-de-sac he had seen on the GPS map but was unable to make out through the blanket of grey that still hung around. There was only one other house on the cul-de-sac as far as he knew, and it had a long drive as well. The cul-de-sac led to a single road that ran parallel with the coast, dividing high end houses along the waterfront with an 18 hole golf course on the inland side. It appeared quiet out there.

Uneasy about the exhaust fumes that were filling the house, Drew left with Bella–returning through the living room and exiting back out of the sliding door into the night.

With the smoke closing in on his path back to the boat, Drew made hasty exit past the pool, down to the lower landing and back out onto the pier.

Midway down the pier, he stopped and looked back

at the house, over to the neighbor's pier, and out on the quite waterway.

"Safe as it is going to get, Bella."

The sky continued to glow pink in the distance as smoke crept along the surface of the water. Drew grabbed Bella and made the leap to the stern of the *Hannah Cole*. With one last look around, Drew dropped into the companionway, secured the batter boards, closed the blackout curtains, and crawled into the comfort of Hannah's v-berth.

Finally able to close his eyes, Drew thought of Joshua Slocum, the first man to solo circumnavigate the globe in a boat named the *Spray*. Rounding the tip of South America, Josh had used carpet tacks scattered on his deck to warn him of boarding indians, cannibals in theory. Here, in the same predicament, Drew had Bella instead of tacks.

Chapter 7

Drew woke the next day, sprung to his feet, grabbed Bella, and climbed out through the companionway into *Hannah*'s cockpit.

"Jesus, how long have we been out?"

His iPhone read 1:17 PM.

The sky was still grey but the smoke was clearing. Visibility was much improved and he could see further down the coastline. Other than the sound of the sea against the hull and the perpetual clanging of his nuisance flag halyard, all was quiet. Soot and ash from the fires had blanketed *Hannah*'s topsides and the condensation caused grey streaks down her hull. She looked like a bombed out mess. Maybe better this way, Drew thought. Sometimes sailors would leave their boats in apparent disrepair while cruising. They would remove their hailing port and fly flags of third world countries to avoid the interest of unsavory characters.

Before crossing the gap over to the floating dock, Drew grabbed some supplies and put binoculars on the scene. The house was quite visible now and the glass of its windows reflected the sky's gloom back at him. There was no activity along the waterway either.

Lowering the binoculars, Drew noticed another floating body. She was caught in the rigging of the piling barge, a heavyset woman in a terrycloth robe. Sea life had nibbled away most of her face and looked to have been working on the bloated, bluing flesh of her enormous, naked breasts.

Drew hopped over to the dock and used a gaff to set the body free.

Looking again out over the water he could see several more corpses floating, bobbing, as they made their way out to sea.

Feeling a little exposed now that there was better visibility, Drew headed with Bella up the pier to the house, constantly keeping watch on the neighbor's pier–another unknown.

Once at the house, Drew took a right this time and went around to the front via the side yard. As the night before, the 1911 was back in hand at the ready and Bella was out ahead of him.

Entering the front yard, he lowered his weapon as he looked down the drive toward the cul-de-sac. Separating him from it was a six foot coquina wall that ran the length of the property, terminating at the wetlands preserve on one end and the sea at the other. It isolated the tip of the peninsula and was bisected only by an equally high automatic gate held firmly in place at the end of the driveway.

"Sometimes you get dealt the right hand," Drew said to Bella who was taking a crap next to a towering, 20 foot tall metal lawn sculpture alongside the drive.

The place did have its disadvantages though. Drew examined the front of the house-all that glass-it was a fishbowl. Any light on inside the house could be seen from the outside as well as any movement.

Staying off to the right, in the security of the live oaks that canopied the yard, Drew made his way down the drive toward the automatic gate. He was glad to see that Bella was staying out of view of its iron rungs as well. With his back against the coquina wall, Drew had to mentally force himself to peek around and through the gate to the cul-de-sac. He had witnessed the relentless energy of the Stage-1s and wasn't so sure one of the neighbors, with bloodshot eyes and blackened teeth, wouldn't be able to vault right over it.

Peering through the bars of the gate, he was able to see out to the greens of the expansive golf course. A pair of club-less golfers were ambling around about two hundred yards away from a golf cart that had been driven into a sand trap. Drew could tell from their movements that they were probably Stage-2s. The head of one of the duffers was cocked dramatically to the right, neck clearly broken.

When they both had their backs to him, Drew craned his head out further to see down the street. About 200 feet away, a little girl, maybe 10, crouched in a smocked dress over a woman's body lying on the asphalt. As she bit chunks of flesh from the woman she would tilt her head back, face toward the sky, and swallow the gore like a baby bird.

Drew swallowed back the vomit coming up in his throat.

Bella spotted the girl, growled, and let out a bark.

The girl turned.

Drew froze, and in a millisecond the girl was on it, sprinting toward the gate. Drew spun and crouched down behind the wall when the girl came slamming into it. Just out of her view, he could see her blood soaked little hands forcing through the gate at Bella who was now in a frenzy of excitement.

"Crooat, croooat," the feeble voiced young one called out to her.

Cover blown, Drew scooped up Bella and dashed back around the side of the house and through the back door he entered the night before.

He rushed across the living room and stared out the front entrance down the drive at the little girl now pacing the fence. She continued with the same croaking noise that Dottie and the sailor had made. She had also attracted the two golfers who were now ambling down the road toward the gate.

"Fuck!" Drew called out, exploding the silence of the house. "We can't make those mistakes again, and Bella, for Christ sakes, what the hell is your problem, cool it with the damned barking."

Bella just looked up at him bright eyed and panting, tongue out, wagging drool onto the oak floors.

Drew looked out the front door pane again. The golfers were just arriving and seemed unsure what the party was about. The little girl however, would pause between pacing and rattle the gate in its track with clenched fists. She seemed to be staring right at him. There was focus there. Good thing was she wasn't getting over that fence, either she physically couldn't or was without reason to understand she possibly could.

"C'mon, go away."

Drew cursed himself for only bringing the .45. The AR was on the boat along with the 9mm Glock and he sure wasn't going back to get them. From this range, he could have probably taken her out with one shot of the rifle. Using the pistol would be a sure miss and multiple gunshots may attract attention.

The infected trio stayed outside the gate for some time. Tiger Woods, as Drew named him, was the slimmer golfer, and

John Daley, the heavyset one, milled about while the girl was still intent on getting through the gate.

Suddenly, out of the range of Drew's view, something caught the girl's attention. Drew could hear her guttural outbursts through the thick mahogany door. She disappeared immediately from view. Tiger and John ambled off after her.

Drew continued to watch until he felt comfortable that they would not return.

"How many of those things were there? How many people were on this island? A thousand? Two thousand? Drew had seen a number of houses on the GPS map. There were also tennis courts and a country club, from what he had been able to tell, and they clearly had to be close by. One thing he did know was there was only one small bridge over to the island. He remembered it from the charts. That probably meant a finite amount of people were here with few, if any, coming or going over that thoroughfare.

Drew inspected the house again now that daylight lit the rooms. It was a showplace. A bit modern and not quite to Drew's taste, but you could certainly appreciate expensive, quality things. As he made his rounds, Drew looked at photographs.

Burt and Mellie Fowler had two daughters, both college graduates. One had gone to Duke and one to UNC Charlotte; there were pictures of both their graduating days. Burt was a retired Judge and Mellie had been a Principle at Port Royal Elementary. They seemed happy enough and had done well for themselves.

Drew thought of Bert, sitting in his dream car, wondering

about his wife, his daughters, and imagining the worst. Drew thought of his own wife and son and understood Burt's urge to turn the ignition of the V8 with the garage doors down.

Drew went into the kitchen. The Sub-Zeros were growing warm now. He rummaged around and pulled out a slab of bacon and some eggs.

"We need some breakfast Bella, whether we feel like it or not."

Drew pulled out a Williams-Sonoma frying pan, found utensils in a drawer, and started to work.

After staring over at the lifeless Keureg, he hunted down some instant coffee, went to the sink and filled up a kettle.

Halfway through, he realized what he was doing.

"What the fuck is wrong with me?" he said, and last night–I was thinking about taking a shower. "God dammit, you are a dead man if you keep up the mistakes," Drew cursed again, slamming the kettle into the sink and startling Bella.

He hauled in a patio chair from outside and posted it in the foyer next to the front door where he and Bella sat eating the eggs and bacon. The coffee he made–from a case of Aquafina he drummed up from the pantry–made him feel more together, certainly more human. Looking out the front door and down the drive there was no more commotion at the gate.

"So, what now?" Drew said, leaning down and rubbing Bella's cheek. That was the question. What was he doing? What had led him here? For the last few days he felt like he had been on autopilot and now he was in some rich guy's house, eating his breakfast, while the guy was in the garage busy stinking up the interior of his classic hotrod.

Drew got up, went to a large white leather sofa in the living room and collapsed into it. Staring at the glass sculpture and family photographs above the mantle, he realized he was trying just to make some normal human contact. He wanted to hear someone again, see someone behaving normally. Sure, one could call him introverted–hell, he was about to attempt a solo circumnavigation. He could do without the people but what he was realizing now was the thought of losing contact forever. That was something that had never crossed his mind. It was terrifying. How many other survivors were out there? Surely this thing had not gone global. He hoped not, but it did seem to have spread rapidly and it was certainly a possibility with today's transportation. So again, what now?

Survive first and make contact second, he thought. For Drew, he defined common sense simply as knowing your resources and understanding how to use them in order to accomplish a task. Task number 1 was simply to survive, to have all the necessities that you need for life. He had all of those. Resources would not be a problem. They seemed endless when he thought of all the houses down the coastline. Less people equaled more available resources. One however, would prove to be an issue. How quick he was to nearly drink from the tap, to bathe in it. How many people would survive days without drinking from the tap until they either went mad and risked it or just absent mindedly had a glass of water, or brushed their teeth? No water unless it came from a bottle was to be trusted unless there was a way to test it. Drew's holding tanks on *Hannah* were full of fresh water he knew to be safe. There were also several cases of bottled water aboard and two cases in the house. If worse came to worse he could capture the rain. Seeking out water would take risk. It would be the goal of any survivor, the commodity, what people would die for.

Drew looked into the bottom of his empty mug. What he felt he needed immediately was more intel. Once more, he was on his feet, scowering the house with new ambition. Rifling through the mail, he found nothing of importance. He grabbed the remote to the TV and hit the power button. "Just checking," he said to Bella. It remained black screen.

Drew found a laptop on a desk in the master bedroom and powered it up. It was Millie's personal computer that clearly had seen very little use and the wireless just remained in the "searching" state. He was running out of ideas.

Back in the kitchen, Drew glanced at the note on the counter again.

"Text me if you need anything."

Shit, why had he not thought of it before? Burt's phone. It was plugged into the Stingray's stereo.

Drew went out to the garage. The fumes had all cleared but it gave way to an odor similar to pumpkins about ready to turn. Drew walked around to the passenger side of the silver corvette and opened the door. He quickly retrieved Burt's phone from the console and made haste back to the living room.

Drew looked at the phone screen at the picture of Burt's family.

Beneath it read, "slide to unlock."

"Fuck," he said, beginning once more to search the house for every possible four number combination that he could find.

No luck.

He slid the phone, what could have been a time capsule of events, into his pocket.

"Speaking of time capsule," Drew said, as he glanced

over into the kitchen at the 26 inch flat screen on the wall. He remembered there was an enormous 60 inch Samsung LED in the master bedroom. Returning there, Drew checked the cabinet beneath it. Sure as shit, a Tevo. He wasn't sure exactly how it worked but it could possibly have been set up to record over the last week. Regardless of the channel, there was a good possibility there was news, or an emergency broadcast, or something.

Removing the Tevo from the cabinet, he unplugged the connection from the TV and sighed, staring at the AC plug. He would have to use the inverted power from his boat.

Just then, shots sounded out in the distance.

"Pop, pop."

Was that? Drew paused, straining his ears for more sounds.

Another "pop" came.

It was gunfire.

Drew ran into the living room, tossed the Tevo on the couch and continued on into the foyer. He could hear a car's motor, revving to redline. The sound was growing louder.

Another "pop, pop" sounded out.

Drew pulled the Colt from his holster as he reached the front door.

Looking through the glass panes, he was just in time to see a white and silver, striped police Dodge charger sedan coming from the direction of the golf course. It skidded and slammed sideways into the coquina wall at the front gate.

"Oh shit," Drew responded as an enormous black police officer stepped out of wrecked vehicle and threw down his pistol. It clattered on the ground. Reaching back into the vehicle, the officer pulled out a pistol grip shotgun and began firing at something out of Drew's line of sight.

Drew slammed the deadbolts open and threw open the front door so hard the glass front nearly shattered.

Pistol out in front of him, Drew ran down the drive and yelled, "Jump the gate."

The cop swung around and took notice of Drew while pointing the shotgun at him. He was in a panic. He turned again and began firing at what now came into Drew's view.

"Oh fuck," Drew said, stopping in his tracks. He could see the ruts that the police car had made coming across the manicured links and there had to be at least 10 Stage-1s sprinting across the fairway of the 14th hole. Off in the distance, he could see maybe 30 Stage-2s, shuffling toward their position.

"The gate, climb on your hood and get your ass over here," Drew called out to him.

"Boom, boom, boom," the officer fired rounds that took off the head of what looked to be a Stepford wife out in front of the pack.

"Boom, Boom," The shotgun roared again, taking down a crazed pest control man in a red mist.

They were on him now.

"Get over here," Drew pleaded, Bella at his side, barking fiercely.

The officer turned, almost having forgotten about Drew. He threw down his weapon and climbed up onto the hood of the cruiser just as a naked teenage boy and a woman in a jogging suite clawed at him and snapped at his legs.

The officer grabbed the top of the gate and began to drag himself over.

Using one foot, he leveraged off of the face of the jogger as the teenager bit through his khaki uniform pants into his calf. The man managed to heave himself over and finally on the other side, staggered as he returned to his feet.

"Run, Drinkers. Run! Lots of Drinkers are coming," The officer warned. "Drinkers?" Drew called out at the approaching policeman. The officer stumbled and went down on one knee. "The ones, the ones that drank the wa…" The officer stumbled again and paused.

As the officer looked up, Drew immediately recognized his eyes had changed and he seemed lethargic as he staggered to his feet. As the officer curled back his lips and exposed his teeth, Drew fired his weapon nearly point blank into the man's forehead as the infection took hold of him.

Drew looked beyond the fence. More of these "Drinkers" had joined the boy and the jogger—who was now in even a bigger tizzy over having her nose crushed in. Despite watching the officer make it over the fence, it appeared that the infected had not figured it out yet.

"Bella, come," Drew said, scooping her up into his arms.

The police cruiser had damaged the gate and it was still holding, but he wasn't going to stick around long enough to find out for how long.

Drew turned and ran back up the drive into the house, slammed the front door shut and threw the latches.

"Fuck! That shit ain't gonna hold either."

Running through the living room and out the back door onto the wooden walkway, halfway to the pool, he stopped, turned around, ran back into the house and to the kitchen.

Just as he turned the last gas burner of the stove on, the first of the creatures slammed against the front door.

"Oh, shit," Drew called out, returning to the living room and catching sight of the Tevo.

"No time," he assured himself as more crashes came

from the front of the house.

Drew exited the rear of the house, rushed around the pool and down the pier to the boat.

He leapt, while tossing Bella midair into the cockpit cushions and then addressed the stern line immediately. Pulling out his line knife, he sliced through the tether and *Hannah* swung gently out into the waterway, still held secure by the piling but apparently out of harm's way.

It startled Drew to see that it was Stage-2s that arrived at the head of the dock first. He was even more surprised to see Stage-2s beginning to amble down the neighboring dock as well. Drew quickly figured that while the Stage-1 (Drinkers, the officer had called them–must have still been busy focusing on the front of the house, the Stage-2s had ignorantly found their way around the side.

Now there was Stage-2 pedestrian traffic all the way down both piers and the first of them made their way out onto the floating dock beside the Pursuit. A soccer mom with a tennis racket bag still slung around her shoulder had one arm dangling uselessly beside her. It had been chewed all the way down to the bone. She too had been apparently eating and had clearly included her two front lips in the meal. A chef arrived, his blood smattered whites and checked pants made him look more like a butcher. There was also a middle aged female Re-max agent Drew saw from the logo at the top of a dangling nametag. A small boy in a tee ball outfit had a broken neck and he seemed to struggle to keep his head turned up.

The sun was going down now as Drew stood on the deck of the *Hannah Cole,* mesmerized by what he was seeing. They were reaching for him, all the while somehow conscious of the watery distance between them and their target, floating 20 feet out on the sailboat. Their frustration amplified their agitation. They snapped their teeth together and glared at him from vacant, milked over eyes.

The neighbor's dock was crowding fast and didn't have a railing. Drew watched as corpses collided, knocking each other into the water. They disappeared beneath the surface almost instantly and did not return to view.

He continued to watch as more Stage-2s crowded the piers. Keeping his eyes on the house, the first Drinker arrived on the scene and began fighting through the herd at the top of the pier.

They must have finally made it into the hou…

Drew flinched and was cut off mid thought as the gas from the stove met the pilot of the fireplace, blowing out the windows of the house with an expanding ball of fire. The live oaks surrounding the home were immediately doused in flames and a plume of smoke began to rise skyward into the air. Even at this safe of a distance, small fragments of the home were landing, splashing in the water around him.

The creatures on the dock turned back toward the inferno as flaming Drinkers fought their way down to the pier, setting several Stage-2s alight as they clawed their way through.

Halfway down the pier, one of the Drinkers, unrecognizable through the flames, stumbled and fell flat. Within seconds, still burning, it got to its feet, slower now, clearly having passed on to the next stage. Drew could see the heat had charred the clothes off its body causing the flesh underneath to cook and split open like a hotdog casing. Seeing the blackened, charred face with professionally maintained teeth crashing together made Drew shudder.

Drew climbed into the cockpit and keyed life into the diesel. Removing the tether from the piling, he was now free and slipped the boat into gear.

The sun was beginning to set low in the horizon as Drew set *Hannah*'s course eastward, back to the sea. In the growing distance, the infected lined the two piers, arms clawing the air before them. They appeared to be waving "Godspeed" as Drew piloted *Hannah* back into the channel.

✥ ✥ ✥

The lack of light from land caused the sky to have to make up the difference as the stars began to illuminate the path out past the last channel markers into the Atlantic. It was getting colder now and the skies had cleared. Only a column of smoke still rising from Port Royal and the new, smaller one in the direction of Cat Island disturbed the brilliance of the planetarium overhead. Drew was shivering but his physical discomfort was being overcome by the emotional.

That cop, he just could not get it out of his head; the man's terror, the confrontation, the change that he so quickly underwent-and oh god, having to pull the trigger on him. Watching the man crumple to the ground at his hand was as hard to overcome as it had been with Dottie. The events played over and over in his head. What was that guy thinking? If he had been just a little quicker, had just moved his leg over an inch this may have played out differently. That cop had answers and more answers than Drew had at this minute.

Drew felt like motoring *Hannah* to the horizon and off

the edge of the world. Instead, well offshore now, he pulled the engine stop and disappeared into the cabin. Coming down the companionway ladder, the thin rectangular housing of Burt's iPhone pressed against his front leg.

Drew pulled it out, plugged it into his charger, and stared at the four empty slots. It instructed, "enter passcode."

With a sigh, Drew passed through the salon door, crawled into the v-berth, and curled up next to Bella.

Chapter 8

Drew's brain continued to churn thoughts from the second he opened his eyes again. It was morning, 9:17 AM, and the sun glowed brilliantly through the cabin deadlights where he sat with Bella, sharing another can of Mary kitchen, piecing together bits of the big puzzle and recording everything in *Hannah*'s ship log.

The officer had called the Stage-1s, Drinkers. Clearly, he meant those that made contact with the water. Was it contact with the water? Or did you have to consume it to turn? This was yet to be answered. Then, there were the Stage-2s. The officer had turned directly into a Stage-2 after being bitten. He died because of the infection and whatever it was had reanimated his body like a grand puppeteer. Drew was under the logical assumption that both stages carried the disease and could spread it, but you could only become a Drinker by contact with the tainted water. It was obvious that these Drinkers had been able to spread the disease quite rapidly–they were still alive and with some cognitive ability, perhaps skewed, but certainly not to be taken for granted. And they were fast moving, whereas Stage-2s tended to possess an out-of-sight, out-of-mind, level of intelligence. When they took notice of a target, they had the same hunger as the Drinkers but were much slower. They were Walkers and they were dead and despite what Fox news had said, a headshot was the only known cure for both phases of the disease.

Drew unfolded his charts and stared at the land masses before him. For there to be lack of communication, lack of air traffic, and lack of response to the carnage he had seen, the disease had to have been planted at strategic locations throughout the country. After that, the Drinkers apparently made quick work of things.

The United States Military had used concept of shock and awe to intimidate the enemy on initial confrontation in the War on Iraq. This disease took advantage of shock and awe and had caused confusion, much in the same way. He had already experienced that first hand. When you had a Drinker tearing toward you, all you wanted to do was get the fuck out of Dodge and seeing the Walkers mope around with their insides on the out was nauseating but mesmerizing.

Just then, Burt's car flashed to mind. "It was a 1962 Corvette, I'm sure of it, round lights with the black grill," Drew said, launching from the settee.

He grabbed Burt's cell and slid the arrow onscreen to unlock. Punching in the numbers 1, 9, 6 and 2, icons suddenly appeared on the screen. "I know my fucking cars," Drew said, winking at Bella. Bella looked back, head cocked and curious as if she were staring into an RCA Phonograph. Drew pressed the Safari icon first. "Safari cannot open this page because your iPhone is not connected to the internet." "Of course." Drew hit backspace several times and only came up with a prior Google search for fishing rod holders. "Shit."

He closed Safari and pressed the email icon. Discouraged, he quickly saw that this was clearly not Judge Burt's business email as the Gmail account was rarely visited. It was full of automatic junk mail from Amazon, Home Depot, iTunes purchase receipts, and miscellaneous life insurance policy fluff. No significant mailings had occurred coming or going over the past week.

The Messages icon offered more promise.

Drew held his breath and pressed the first of five text messages. It was a group message, started by his wife, and included Burt and his two daughters.

"Burt, the girls are not responding to me and I'm worried about what I just saw on the news. I am trying to call, please pick up the phone." -Millie

Again, "Burt, please pick up the phone." -Millie

"Sorry, I was in the shower. What is going on? Are you safe? I just turned on the TV." -Burt

Then there was a 15 minute gap. Drew checked the phone log and saw that Burt had spoken verbally with his wife.

Then the texts started again…

"Millie, I tried calling back and you wouldn't answer. Did you get out of there?" -Burt

"Millie you are worrying me." -Burt

"Sorry, I had to hang up because I didn't want them to hear me." -Millie

"Where are you now? Did you make it out of there?" -Burt

"No, we are still here. I made it into the back office with Julie. Those things are in the studio. I'm scared Burt. They came through the front glass. Three of them jumped on Alice. They were biting her." -Millie

"Stay put! I am coming over there." -Burt

"No Burt, it's not safe. I think we are ok now. The office door is locked and they have not discovered us. Don't leave Burt, promise me. It won't do me any good if anything happened to you." -Millie

"I just called Chief Johnson over at the police station and got no answer. I am still working on getting someone to you. This is apparently happening at several other places in the country. Every TV channel is broadcasting the news but some local stations have apparently already dropped off the air. This is bad, Mil. Please stay where you are. I am working on it." -Burt

"Girls, please respond, your dad and I have to know that you are ok." -Millie

"Tried calling mom, she is not responding either." -Burt

"Julie thinks we can stand on a desk and crawl up onto the roof. There is a hatch." -Millie

"Do that. Do it now if you can but be careful." -Burt

"We made it up. Right now we are on the roof of the studio. Everyone has gone crazy. There are people getting attacked. I saw Mel Genest bite Mrs. Collins on the neck. He killed her and she got back up. She is walking around in the street. She see's me up here. They know we are up here. They are all looking up here. There is lots of screaming. It is terrible. I'm so scared." -Millie

"Girls! Where are you?" -Millie

"Millie, stay calm, I am sure the girls are ok. They are smart. You know they are figuring something out." -Burt

"A man came running down the street and Mrs. Collins grabbed him. She is eating him Burt. Promise me you won't go outside. Is the gate closed?" -Millie

"Yes, it is closed. I can hear sirens but I am not seeing

anything here. Don't worry about me I just need you to stay safe." -Burt

"We should be ok, those things can't seem to find a way up here. Julie was able grab her bag on the way up here so we have a little food and water. We will sit tight." -Millie

"Ok, I have been trying to call everyone. I am going to try and call Chief Johnson again now." -Burt

"Julie says she isn't feeling well, she looks very bad." -Millie

"Millie, Stay away from her!!!!" -Burt

"Millie." -Burt

"Millie!" -Burt

"Millie, answer me!" -Burt

"Millie please answer me." -Burt

Drew looked up from the phone and stared out of the companionway toward the open ocean. It looked as desolate as he felt.

He checked the individual texts to the two daughters and the Chief of Police. There was only pleading for response on Burt's end. It was hard to read. Burt had been a good man.

Drew read on, this time the texts were with an attorney in San Francisco. Clearly the two had been discussing something called Guardian Ad Litem and then the conversation had changed.

There were video texts.

"Burt, a fucking plane just crashed outside my office," -Sloan Wilkerson

There was a video taken through the blinds of Sloan Wilkerson's office that lay high on a hill in downtown San Francisco with a breathtaking view out over the bay. About a quarter of a mile away, an airplane fuselage lay inverted and burning in the street. Split in the middle, the wings had torn free and engulfed several buildings on fire along its path.

Drew played it again.

Focusing on the plane, what the attorney probably had not noticed while taking the video, were the several different fires erupting far out on the hillside and the Drinkers off in the distance that were racing up the street.

"Sloan, turn on the news. The world has gone to shit. Millie is trapped in the back room of a Yoga Studio. People have gone mad and are on some sort of a murderous rampage." -Burt

"Fuck man, there are some outside my office. I see them now. They are here too." -Sloan Wilkerson

There was another video. It showed the back wall of Sloan's office that was made mostly of glass block, it wrapped around in a semicircle that backed up to a main street. Through it you could clearly see the distorted images of the figures clawing at it from the outside.

"Holy Christ," you could hear Sloan say as the video came to an end.

That was the last message with Sloan Wilkerson.

The last text conversation was with a man named Ernie Chamberlain. Checking the contacts list, Drew saw that he worked for the Department of Homeland Security. Clearly a longtime intimate friend from another life, Burt had been the one to reach out.

"Burt here, I have run into a situation here with my wife. I know it isn't your gig and I know you are probably busy with what is apparently going on, but I need some possible help here on Cat Island." -Burt

"Burt, been on vacation. Things are not going well where I am either. I can tell you that there is no hope to be had. That is all I can say." -Ernie Chamberlain

"Where are you?" -Burt

"Stuck with my wife on the London eye. We won't be getting off." -Ernie Chamberlain

"Dear God, I am sorry." -Burt

"It is a beautiful view at least. Gotta sign off for now to save battery power. I wish you the best." -Ernie Chamberlain

That was the last message with Ernie.

A million thoughts circulated in Drew's mind as he set down the phone, opened his pilot's log, and made record.

Current position approx 21 nautical miles off the coast of St Catherine's island, Georgia. Feeling boxed in. Destination unknown. He closed the book, grabbed his coastal charts and headed out on deck.

"Fuck," he said, recalling the last text. London. Where to now? The Bahamas? Costa Rica? Puerto Rico? Hell, how's Cuba holding up for fucks sake?" Currently equipped, he was free to go anywhere and that had been the plan. So where to now? It really didn't make all that much sense to head to some remote location. His resources would run out eventually and heading to a place that was low on resources to begin with was a bad idea.

He looked out at the open ocean and maddeningly clear, blue sky.

If he pulled the EPIRB out there who would come? Shit, if he pulled the EPIRB here, two miles from the coast of South Carolina, who would come? He stared toward the shoreline. He needed to think, to clear his head, regain focus, and formulate a plan. For now, he would hug the coast and let the wind and current take him south.

⁜ ⁜ ⁜

Once secured to a jack line, Bella paced the decks inspecting a trio of Dolphins that had been escort from the time *Hannah* first had cloth in the air. The conditions had been perfect and *Hannah* flew south wing-to-wing making quick time. Drew hardly noticed. He sat on the cockpit bench and steered the tiller with his foot, nose buried in the charts.

"Crack!"

It was the unmistakable sound of a single gunshot that caused Drew to spring to his feet. He had not noticed the large catamaran off of his bow, approximately half a mile ahead.

Drew immediately slammed the tiller to port and the boat jibed hard to starboard, maintaining safe distance from the warning.

He grabbed the handheld VHF.

"Sailing vessel to my port, this is the *SV Hannah Cole*, acknowledging your signal. I mean you no harm, over," he hailed.

There was no response on 16.

He tried again.

No response.

Lifting his binoculars, he could see the catamaran had also changed course. Soon, it disappeared out of view.

Not too friendly, Drew thought.

Bella glanced up in response to the commotion and then back down as one of the Dolphins came up for air.

This exchange with the catamaran was troubling. It had to have clearly seen the sails in the air and known there was a competent individual at the helm but didn't want to make contact. Sailors were usually a warm, tight knit group. That was part of the appeal. Humans were strange animals though. Even the most predictable people can act against their character when under stress and Drew understood they could be dangerous.

On a new course and the shore more visible now, Drew kept his eyes on the coastline. He could see smoke rising from several populated areas as he pressed south but he had seen no further signs of humanity.

It was midafternoon and Drew was clipping along, just off of the north coast of Cumberland Island, when he first spotted the cruise ship through his binoculars. At first he was not quite sure what he was looking at. It was nearly an hour later when he was close enough to get a better understanding of the massive structure that had been interrupting the horizon.

Drew was getting what would normally be a bird's eye view of the entire topsides as she lay on her side, decks nearly at a 90 degree angle to the sea. Over the past several days, the wind and tide clearly nudged her gradually higher and higher into the shallow waters at the south end of Cumberland.

At this distance, Drew could see that it was one of the "Funships," clearly one of Carnival's fleet because of the huge red wing now jutting up from the ocean. He also saw that she had dumped a large number of her passengers into the shallow coastal waters as there were quite a number of figures ambling around on the beach.

Approaching with caution and keeping close eye on his depth, Drew doused the sails and brought the diesel back to life.

Still safely offshore, he proceeded to the massive stern rising out of the ocean. Spilled oil and Diesel made colorful, toxic, blossoms on the surface of the water around him as he made his way through a stew of deck furniture and other debris. A yellow water slide, once carrying giggling kids into the currently emptied rear pool was now a twisted mess and terminated into the sea. It was horrific and breathtaking at the same time.

Rounding the stern, he could clearly make out "Carnival *Fa*," scrolled on the transom. The *Fascination*.

Drew swung *Hannah* wide around the *Fascination*'s rudder to the bottom side of the wreck, careful to avoid *Hannah*'s mast spreaders making contact with one of the ship's massive propellers, towering high overhead.

He checked his depth again and the display read that he was safely in 47 feet of water.

Circling around, he came alongside the ship, keeping *Hannah*'s bow out to sea. He wanted to give the cockpit and companionway a view of the shoreline. Safe in the downstream eddy of the ship, Drew put out bumpers to port and secured *Hannah*'s stern lines to the massive aluminum anti-galvanic corrosion plates bolted to the bottom of the *Fascination*'s welded hull.

The sea had settled into slight chop and the sun was setting behind the live oaks of Cumberland Island, slowly turning the lights out on its new inhabitants. Once a diverse range of all walks of life, age, wealth and beauty, this group milling about on shore could now be divided into just two categories, Drinkers and Walkers.

Clearly aware of his presence, there had to be at least 200

of them prowling around, frustrated by the 100 yards of water or so that separated them from Drew's position. It was curious to see people in bathing suits so reluctant about the water, but they were. Since they had waded onto the beach in their exodus from the fallen ship, they chose to remain ashore and had not been overcome by the temptation to approach Drew and Bella. This was comforting.

Suddenly, there was movement at the south end of the beach and Drew spotted it at the same time as several of the Drinkers. A quarter mile down the beach, two wild horses had emerged from the trees and out onto the sand.

Having been rulers of their island for years and confident in their power, they made a tragic mistake of underestimating the infected ghouls that were running in their direction. They just stood there looking up at the approaching Drinkers.

It was a deeply tanned man in Bermuda shorts and a Hawaiian shirt (he could have been a pool bartender) that dug into the first one.

The horse reared as his companion exploded off of the beach and back into the trees.

Even at this distance, Drew could hear the whinny of the massive animal as a second Drinker, a peacock of a male in his mid-20s, assisted in bringing the horse to the ground.

Within seconds it was over, the crowd had shifted and the Walkers began to amble down the beach where there was a fresh kill to take part in. All focus on Drew was now gone. It was dark and the beach began to clear as the infected disappeared into the tree line in search of more food.

✤ ✤ ✤

Drew was exhausted and Bella too, for that matter. With *Hannah* safely nestled against the massive cruise ship, he grabbed the little Chihuahua and disappeared through the companionway and collapsed in the pilot berth below.

The overall stillness of the cabin amplified the strained, metallic, groans of the wrecked vessel as it continually adjusted to its new placement on the ocean floor. There were other noises. Noises deep within the hull that made Drew cover his ears as he fought to get needed rest. Whether coherent survivors or the infected, those trapped inside relentlessly and desperately struggled for freedom with no chance of hope. Even Bella seemed to shift in her sleep, frequently raising her head at the sounds of clanging that persisted through the night.

Chapter 9

It was mid-morning and Bella woke first. Drew stirred next at the sound of her barking.

"Shhh, hush, what is it girl?"

Then he heard it, a small outboard. It was approaching.

Scrambling to his feet, he scooped up Bella, snatched up the .45, and leapt through the companionway into the cockpit.

"Well, well, well, look what we have here. Good morning Dorothy. I think you will agree now that you aren't in Kansas anymore. You and your little dog too, that is, and you can put the gun away now," Shark said, pulling a small Zodiac beside *Hannah* before shutting off its little 8hp Mercury.

Drew stood there in astonishment as he looked down at the man smiling up at him.

Shark was clearly stoned out of his mind and wearing what looked to be a ragged blue Union soldier's uniform blouse and an ancient light blue pair of pants with a stripe running down the side. What in the hell is up with this guy? Drew thought.

"Look, if you follow me, I can help you put *Hannah* here on a mooring ball. There is somewhere safe for you and your little Muffie."

"It's Bella," Drew corrected him, still in disbelief.

"Of course it is. Well, you and Bella follow me. You are free to say no, but we could use your help," Shark said, firing up the outboard.

"Where?" Drew yelled, but was unheard as Shark motored away.

"Keep it on 16," Shark called out over his shoulder.

"Fuck," Drew said in resignation, climbing out to the bow and untying his lines.

He turned the ignition, stirring *Hannah* to a gentle rumble and headed out after Shark. Within 20 minutes they rounded the jetties into Cumberland Sound, between Cumberland and Amelia Islands. As they passed the northern tip of Amelia, Drew was taken aback by what he saw. A red brick fortification loomed in the distance.

Drew raised his binoculars and inspected the long walls and massive bastians. Standing atop one of the bastians was a couple of what looked to be Union soldiers hurling a body over the wall onto the beach below.

As they passed the massive fort, Drew looked ahead to the Zodiac as Shark held his arm high, fingers in the V of a peace sign in response to the waving men at the fort.

Drew's handheld radio cracked to life.

"Welcome to Fort Clinch. We will be back after getting you settled. But first, I have some business in town, over," Shark came across.

Shark pressed on, guiding Drew around and down the Amelia River on the western side of island where he helped put *Hannah* on a mooring ball just outside the City of Fernandina Beach.

"You should be all set," Shark said, pulling alongside

Drew and helping him with his fenders. He motioned over to a familiar boat on the hook, just yards away, *Minerva*.

"She's been here a couple of days and nothing has happened to her. This place is all pretty much a total loss and those things are not too interested in sailing from the looks of it, so *Hannah* here isn't going anywhere."

From their location, Drew looked out upon the town to the city marina. There was octagonal looking building, Brett's Waterway Café the sign read. There was also a City Marina Bait and Tackle store. Just beyond, was a long main street that ran through the center of the 19th century town. Small shops and eateries lined both sides. There were hordes of the infected, both Drinkers and Walkers, swarming the area like ants in a disturbed mound.

Since the moment Bella had stirred him that morning with all the barking, Drew felt again like he was on autopilot. There was relief of being in the presence of another sane (well, seemingly so) member of the human race. Now he was beginning to snap out of it. Who was this guy? He was acting like they were long time friends. Trusting this guy may be a roll of the dice he concluded looking back at the man now offering up a fresh packed bowl of weed.

"Here, pull on this, it will put hair on your chest and clear your head."

"I'm good," Drew responded, declining the generous offer.

"Suit yourself, just means more for me. I see you got that little pea shooter there. If there are more weapons aboard, grab them up and hop aboard–and don't forget little Toto."

Shark lifted his handheld VHF pressed the button.

"Our sailing friend is secure. Running those errands we discussed and then headed back to you, over," Shark radioed.

"Roger that, hurry up though, as you know we got our hands full back here," a man's voice replied. Drew could here gunshots in the background.

The appeal of joining other survivors outweighed the mistrust he had for Shark. Drew began unloading weapons and ammunition down into the little zodiac and hopped aboard with Bella. He looked back at *Hannah*, hoping he had made the right decision as the zodiac sped its way toward the city marina. Straight into what looked to be the center of hell.

"Where the fuck we are going?" Drew said, looking over at Shark and feeling a lump in his throat as they approached the masses of Drinker's now congesting the city marina docks. The infected had responded to the sound of the Zodiac skipping across the water and lined the waterway with impatient hunger.

Shark pointed at a large building painted in several different shades of pastel on the other side of the road from the marina.

Hampton Inn the sign on top read.

Drew hadn't noticed before, the woman and young man that were up on the roof. They were signaling them, having taken notice of their small boat from all of the commotion it was causing.

"How do you propose we…?" Drew questioned.

Shark cut him off and pointed to the boxcars below them.

"The trains," he said.

There was a pair of tracks running next to the Hotel and a train carrying boxcars was pulled alongside the building. Drew's eyes followed the length of the trains and immediately he understood what Shark had planned.

"Oh god, you got to be kidding me," Drew said.

Shark brought the Zodiac into the southern side of the marina. The infected had crowded the docks so thickly now they began to fall over the sides, vanishing below the water's surface.

Lemmings, Drew thought as they pulled alongside a vacant stretch of pier next to a boat ramp. It jutted out from a small, red, shack of a building with an oxidized sign that read "Atlantic Seafood."

Drew tied Bella secure in the Zodiac as Shark grabbed the small boat's painter and stepped onto the pier, securing the line to a cleat.

"Up there," Shark said, and pointed to the top of the seafood store.

Drew nodded in understanding, handing the Mossberg 12 gauge and a large duffel bag to Shark before joining him on the pier.

Bella was pissed she had been left behind and was angrily barking by the time Drew and Shark reached the rooftop.

A large box truck on the other side of the building had the same "Atlantic Seafood" logo printed in faded letters on the side. The top of the truck only partially made up for the gap between their position and the closest box car. A power line running from the top of the store to a utility pole on the other side of the tracks made up the difference.

Surrounding them on three sides was a collection of infected so thick that no square inch of ground could be seen.

One of the Drinkers in particular caught Drew's eye.

"Fuck me," Drew uttered as his head began to spin. It was a hippy chick in her mid-twenties staring up at him. Her ankle length dress was torn and muddied and she wore a Baby Bjorn around her front. At some point in time she had turned and sank her teeth into the soft unformed fontanels of the babies head. The now hollowed out bowl of the child's skull was filled with gore. Its arms and legs were long missing.

Shark took her out with a round from the Mossberg and slung the duffel bag over his shoulder.

"Let's get going," he called out.

One after the other, they went hand over hand out on the power line until they were over one of the rusted boxcars where they dropped down onto the train.

The infected were working themselves into frenzy, reaching up at them as they ran along, jumping the gaps between the boxcars on their way to the hotel.

Standing directly below the hotel sign that loomed above, an attractive redhead that must have been in her early forties and a younger blonde kid in his early twenties leaned out over the top edge of the Hotel's facade.

Drew looked up. "Dude, it's much too high," he said.

Just as he got the words out, Shark unzipped the duffel and pulled out a spear fishing gun.

"Stand back," he called up to the pair above.

They moved clear.

Shark pulled the trigger and the bolt arced high over the top of the building, trailing a thin line behind it.

Quickly, he tied the line to the end of a ½ rope that lay coiled in the duffel.

Shark turned and winked at Drew, "I got this shit."

Within seconds, the blonde kid immediately hoisted up the rope.

Drew was impressed to see how fast the pair was able to make it back down. Malnourished and clearly dehydrated, they fought through it and were soon standing safely on top of the boxcar beside Shark and Drew.

"No time for introductions, we need to head out," Shark said, and led the group down the length of train back toward the seafood market. The infected remained in pursuit alongside them the entire way.

Shark stopped when they arrived back at the power line that was now several feet over their heads.

"What else you got in that bag of tricks, Spiderman?" Drew said.

"Hadn't completely worked that one out yet," Shark returned, staring at the line above, the infected, and their path out of there via the market rooftop.

"Shit. Ok, you guys lie flat so they can't see you. I will draw them away. Once I do, hop down and haul ass back over to that box truck," Drew said.

Before anyone could contest it, he turned and started running back down the train again toward the hotel.

"Down here you dumb bastards," he called out clanging the stock of the spear gun against the steel boxcars as he ran.

It was working. The mob turned away, eyes locked on him and they followed. Looking over his shoulder, Drew could see the trio climb down the side of the boxcar, run across the street, and within seconds, were standing, watching safely from roof of Atlantic Seafood.

When he saw that everyone had made it, he hurled the spear gun out into the crowd, spun around, and bolted back down the length of the train.

The Drinkers were not fooled for long and once more were at his heels just below him. As he ran, he could see the eyes of those standing on the roof go wide when he made the leap far into the void between the boxcar and the safety of the rooftop. He closed his eyes and felt the thick electric cable meet the palms of his hands as they closed around it. He had been able to make purchase at the low spot where the cable sloped down to the rooftop where his group awaited. He shimmied along, out of the reach of the grasping horror below.

"You are one crazy sonofabitch you know that?" Shark said as they scrambled off the roof and back onto the pier below.

"Yea, sometimes you just got to make a decision and go with it," Drew replied, as they piled into the Zodiac.

Firing up the little Mercury, Shark guided them out through the infested marina into the open water.

The woman began to cry. Her eyes puffy and swollen, she leaned over and kissed Shark on the cheek then put her arms around Drew's neck. Shark made eye contact with Drew and winked.

"Thank you guys so much," the blonde kid spoke up as the little RIB sped out into the open water.

"I'm Jeff Jordan and this is my mom, Elizabeth."

"I... I... didn't think we were going to get down from there," Elizabeth sobbed, looking back at the hotel fading in the distance. "You guys risked your lives to get us."

"At your service," Shark replied, lightening the mood with a quick bow. He opened a side compartment and handed out several bottles of water.

Drew looked at the Shark and for the first time realized that the strung out pot head had probably just rescued him as well.

Chapter 10

They rode in silence the rest of the trip. Elizabeth held Bella in her lap and rested her head on Jeff's shoulder as the Zodiac skimmed across the water around the north side of the island to a small isolated beach. It was protected on both sides by mounds of oyster beds, just outside of the northernmost bastion of Fort Clinch.

"Honey, I'm home," Shark said over the handheld and smiled proudly over at his catch of the day.

Within seconds, two older gentlemen in Union dress appeared at the top of the bastian and threw over a rope ladder.

Once at the top, Drew could see that the fort was a pentagon in shape. The surrounding walls were made up of an outer red brick wall that was about three feet thick with an inner earthen wall and a pathway that ran the length between the two as they terminated at each of the five bastians. The walled structure surrounded a large parade ground, skirted by a brick two story barracks off to the right, and another large brick building directly in front of them that faced a front entrance sally port.

Their current location provided an excellent view out over Cumberland Sound. From this angle, Drew could clearly see over the jetty to the cruise ship *Fascination*, lying beached like an enormous whale.

"Saw you come in last night from the very spot where you are standing," Shark nudged Drew.

One of the men in uniform interrupted. He was a tall and trim bearded gentleman in his sixties with thick grey hair and wise but kind eyes. Despite his age, his skin was thick, tough and deeply tanned from sun exposure. He clenched a cigar in his teeth as he spoke.

"My name is Major Nate Williams and this is Sergeant Bill Sloan," he said, introducing the balding, heavyset man who held out his hand.

Drew took it, thinking to himself that Sergeant Bill's jolliness and snow white beard reminded him of Santa.

Jeff and Elizabeth also made their introductions.

"Sergeant Bill, be a good man and take these folks to the infirmary and have Rose take a look at them," Major Nate said. "We have plenty of space for everyone. Ma'am you and your son can take the main section of the officer's quarters to yourselves. It's the penthouse floor of the barracks," he chuckled, "May it suit your needs."

Drew realized this guy was stuck in character. A retired war vet and now tour guide, he had clearly taken the job seriously. There was something quite endearing about it–so was the fact that Sergeant Bill was playing along.

"Shark, we have had activity at the front gate all day, head over with me," Major Nate said.

Shark issued him a respectful salute and the two men departed out from the top of the bastian and up along the high earthen wall that defended the ocean side with enormous defunct cannons.

Sergeant Bill lead Elizabeth, Jeff, and Drew down a steep spiral brick staircase through the center of the bastian and down a long connecting tunnel out to the large parade ground. Still on the job, he gave a brief tour along the way.

"The United States government started construction on this site in 1847 where it housed troops during the Civil and Spanish American wars. Those arched tunnels you see lead from these parade grounds directly to the five bastions and storage areas. The various structures you see in the courtyard include a jail, the barracks, a blacksmith shop, an infirmary, an officer's quarters, and cooking facilities. It's all pretty much how it was back in 1847 minus some electrical and cistern work that's been done."

Drew looked around and saw two more men in blue period uniforms skirt down the arched tunnels into the darkness.

Toward the east wall, a teenage boy in ratty jeans and a flannel shirt was being instructed by another Union Officer in a wheelchair on a hand pump that protruded from the ground.

"That is Colonel Wilcox. He's a crazy old coot, been here the longest and has a big heart. What they are working on there is our bread and butter. That old pump has been providing fresh water to this place since the first bricks were laid. Still works. Water comes from one of the many cisterns around the infrastructure. It just needs a little maintenance every now and then and the Colonel is passing that torch to the young fella there, Josh is his name.

Josh was camping in the park with his family when this thing hit. His parents were lost and he and his sister, Rose, were just able to make it through the gate before we shut it," Sergeant Bill paused. "The Colonel has really taken to the two of them and has been trying to keep their minds off of their loss. He has been giving the two of them tasks and such."

"How many survivors are there?" Drew asked, as they reached the top of a flight of stairs that ran up the left side of the building that lay central to the parade ground. They were standing just outside of the infirmary.

Working fingers on both hands and muttering to himself, Sergeant Bill made the calculation,

"Including the three of you, 16. Two days ago we were at 15 but there was an incident, just inside the gate."

Suddenly, the door to the infirmary opened and a pretty, blonde, fifteen year old girl in dirty jeans and Billabong hooded sweatshirt held it open for them. She smiled at the sight of Bella.

"Anyhow, Rose will take care of you from here. And please, if there is anything you need, don't be shy," Sergeant Bill said, smiling through strained eyes.

He descended back down the stairs and made his way across the parade ground to where the Colonel was still discussing the pump with Josh.

The infirmary was a large, dusty, unsophisticated room with raw, hardwood floors. Two bunk beds with dingy, straw filled mattresses stood against one wall and at other side of the room was a fireplace that seemed to be providing more light than warmth. Shelves along the walls held minimal supplies; miscellaneous prescription medications, two automotive med kits, blankets, sheets, a government issue medical kit, several rolls of toilet paper, and a Philips portable AED (probably a requirement for every state park).

Bella curled up at the hearth of the fireplace as the

newcomers sat down at a wooden table in the center of the room. Rose ladled bowls soup from a kettle on an electric hotplate that was powered by a small Honda Generator that hummed along on the outside of the building.

"I heard Sergeant Bill talking about me and Josh outside the door, about our parents. It's cool. I mean, I'm alright and everything. That is the way it goes right?" Rose said.

The trio remained silent.

She continued, "Major Nate is pretty cool, made me the nurse here, nurse and quartermaster." Rose went to the wall and retrieved some cream for the scrape Julie had received on her arm from the descent off the hotel roof. "Not sure how I am at nursing but my mom was one, so I kinda inherited the job. As far as the quartermaster thing, I guess you could say I am in charge of this building," Rose said proudly. "Below this infirmary is the general store and next to that are the supply rooms. There is plenty of clothing in there to replace what you are wearing. I don't mean to be rude but it looks like you could use it, along with a good shower. Max and Jason rigged one up for us in the old bakery by the Barracks. It isn't fancy but there is plenty of hot water."

"Well thank you Miss Rose, it is much appreciated," Elizabeth said, smiling graciously.

"It seems pretty safe here," Jeff began.

"Yeah, now it is, only a couple of those things were able to slip through when the front gate was shut. Josh and I just made it right behind Sam and Martha who were our neighbors in the campground that's just outside the fort." Rose paused, checking her work on Elizabeth's arm. "Josh and I were in our trailer when we heard a lot of screaming outside. I can't remember much, just the screaming and people running, so we did too. We all ran to the fort. Those things were behind us. I turned and saw that one of them had jumped on my Mom."

Drew could see she was having difficulty.

Rose continued, "Sam and Martha were standing out front in the parking lot and saw us running with those things chasing. We all ran inside the fort and some of them got in. They started biting people. It was the first time I had seen something like that. Thankfully, Jason and Billy were able to shut the gate at the entrance. Buddy had a pistol and started shooting at them. That's all I really remember. Josh and I just kept running across the field into one of those tunnel things. We went up one of those circle staircases and hid out up–top."

"So that's the only way in? The front sally port?" Drew asked.

"Yeah, and it's pretty secure now that the gates are shut. All the walls around us are too high for them to get over. There are windows all around to see out but they are like too skinny for those things to get in. All they can do is just press their arms through," Rose shuddered.

The door to the infirmary opened and a woman in a remarkably clean, khaki park ranger uniform stepped in. At 50 or so years old, she was extremely fit and Drew could tell by the way she carried herself that she was a no nonsense type woman. Her short cropped white hair said she meant business.

Major Nate stepped in behind her.

"This is…" Major Nate began, but the woman cut him off.

"Eileen Simmons," she said, stepping forward, giving everyone a firm handshake. "Welcome to Fort Clinch State Park. Normally our visitors enter through the front gate but in this instance I will let this one slide," she joked, trying to get a smile out of the crowd. I'm sure Nurse Rose has taken care of you nicely," she said. Eileen winked at Rose who leaned against a bed frame and played with her hair. "I don't mean to make such brief introduction but it is getting dark and I would like to show you to your quarters. Crystal is cooking up something for dinner and you will get to meet the rest of the Motley Crew if you will join us tonight."

As they filed out of the infirmary, Major Nate pulled Drew aside, "Walk with me son."

Bella followed, sniffing out the parade ground as Major Nate led Drew up an earthen ramp to the terreplein above the front sally port.

The sunset was brilliant from this vantage point, fiery pinks and deep turquoises; it was utterly stunning and peaceful and a direct contrast to what Major Nate wanted Drew to see on the other side of the wall.

Beneath them, there was a wooden bridge that crossed from the front gate over an empty moat. The bridge led to road that diverged into three branches across a large field. One path led out to the ocean, one led to a visitor parking lot, and a more substantial road lead to the gift shop and museum to the southwest.

The area was teaming with the infected. The moat, perhaps once filled with water was now filled with Drinkers gathered 10 feet deep around the front gate. Walkers by the hundreds filled the fields and lined the outer walls of the fortress from where the oyster beds protected the small beach where they landed. Drew noticed several of the Walkers were also in period uniform but said nothing about it.

Rose had been right, they were not getting in but the infected certainly knew that there were people inside and they were not going to let up.

"It's like they smell us in here," the Major said. "Those fast sons-of-bitches seem to draw the dead ones to us–like goddam bird dogs. It was those bastards that went through my men. The day it happened we were formed up 30 strong, just out there where the roads diverge," Major Nate continued, pointing. "We broke ranks as soon as the first one of those things came out of the woods and attacked my guidon bearer. More came and men started falling. We fell back to the fort and were joined by others fleeing from the camping area. I believe it was Eileen that was last across the bridge, she came from the direction of the gift shop there. It was a blur, worse than anything I had ever seen in my time with the army. Thank god we were able to get the gates shut before the mass of them hit. Six of my men were taken down right in the parade ground before Buddy's pistol ended it all." The Major lit a cigar. "Look Drew, I have five of my original men left: Bill Sloan, Daryl Stephenson, Jason Freeman, Carey Douglas, and Max Dipace. Then there is Buddy Parker, and of course, Shark. I need more heavy lifters and really could use your help around here. You are of course welcome to stay or welcome to go but it would be nice to see you stay."

Drew looked over at the seagulls that lined the outer rampart, many with their eyes closed and bellies full from feasting off of the monsters below. They rested quiet and content.

Drew turned his eyes out to the darkened field, the sea of bodies relentlessly searching for a way in.

He looked out at the black sea and noticed several lights on the horizon.

"I'm in, Major," Drew answered without another thought. "About your men though," Drew asked, "There was an incident a couple days ago at the gates?"

"It's been a long day," The Colonel began to reply when Shark walked up.

"So, is he with us?" Shark piped in, patting the Major playfully on the back. Once again, Drew could tell he was high as a kite.

"Looks like it," Major Nate said, and nodded a thank you to Drew as he blew a cloud of cigar smoke into the air. "Gentlemen, let's get something to eat."

"Ok, but first I would like to see this gate."

The trio descended from the terreplein down the western ramp back onto the parade ground where they passed between two overhanging breezeways. Between them, the long lantern lit, arched brick corridor of the sally port led to a gate, guarded by a bear of a man that appeared to be in his mid-thirty's. He stood smoking a cigarette as a clumsy, awkward looking guy sat on a stone bench off to one side, tying his brogans. Both men were in uniform armed with only a pair of black powder rifles. Behind them was a massive black saloon-door style gate that fastened in the middle with a thick chain and padlock. The infected were in an uproar reaching and clawing between the gaps and bars of the gate, inches from the toy soldiers.

Drew was not surprised to see they were all Drinkers and the noise they created inside the tunnel was torturous. As they approached the soldiers, Drew could see they had little yellow earplugs in.

"Christ, between the noise and the smell," Drew said, putting the back of his hand to his nose.

"Gentlemen, I would like you to meet Mr. Drew McFarland," Major Nate introduced.

The guy with the cigarette bounced it off a Drinker's forehead and put out his hand.

"Max Dipace, good to meet you."

Adjusting the rifle on his shoulder, he sized Drew up. Drew could see this guy was smart and tuff. With his Buddy Holley glasses and rolled pants legs, he was a hipster in Union dress.

The shoe tier stood up from the crate. An Ogre, probably in his late twenties, Drew calculated.

"I'm Carey Douglas, these things are something else, huh," he said, motioning over his shoulder to the Drinkers.

Drew could see the guy's poor hygiene had had taken hold years before the world's current predicament. Drew figured if the Union army had a Gomer Pyle, this was the probably the guy.

"Is that going to hold?" Drew said, as he inspected the 19th century hinged framework that was anchored into the brick.

"Haven't had any issues yet. Lots of force against that gate but it could probably take ten times that amount. The bridge on the other side is a swing bridge, hinged in the middle, not that you can see with those fucks in the way. Anyway, I have been trying to work out a way to get it raised," Max said.

"I'm sure it's hard to make it budge with those assholes standing on it," Drew commented.

"That gate was made a long time ago. Back then they made shit real strong. Nope, don't make things like they used to," Carey piped in, looking the gate up and down as if for the first time.

"Sometimes takes him a while to catch up but he always gets there in the end," Major Nate said. "One of my most dedicated men," he continued, winking at Carey.

Carey was beaming.

"We have been watching the gate in six hour shifts, two people on at all times," Major Nate said, raising his voice over the croaking of the Drinkers who seem to be in competition to be heard. "We also try and have two men up on the wall at all times. We are fortunate that the secluded beach you came in on allows us to only have to concentrate mainly on the front ramparts. It has been a few days now, but we have not had any breaches along our walls or bastions. I like to think we are pretty secure here. Our main concern now is supplies." The Major continued, motioning with a finger to head back down the corridor away from the noise, "Weapons and food: with those two things, I believe that we will be able to survive this. Shark and Daryl have been kind enough to make some good recoveries from the cruise liner debris–the low hanging fruit as it were. Now their plan is to venture further out."

"Me and D are like the marines baby, search and destroy," Shark said, flexing his cabled arms and smiling. He kissed a bicep.

They were back onto the parade ground now and watched in the dusk as Josh and the Colonel prepared to lower the parade ground flag.

"Everyone is beginning to find their place here now," said Major Nate, saluting as the flag came down.

"Major, I hadn't noticed before but what is on that flag?" Drew asked, looking at the period American flag with a circular cluster of stars. Something had been hastily painted in white in the middle of the ring.

"That is a nine painted in the center," Major Nate explained. "Since 1562 this Island has had the flags of 8 nations flown over it.

Josh and the Colonel came up with a 9th.

Chapter 11

Drew knew immediately upon entering that the kitchen had probably always been the fort's true epicenter since its inception. A middle aged, heavy set, dark haired woman wearing a flowered, ankle length dress, tended a wood burning fireplace that warmed the room and simmered a thick stew, steaming in a cast iron pot. The fire flickered dancing shadows on the brick walls with a soft red glow providing the only light the room needed to make the place feel inviting.

The smell of the stew, in combination with the smells of cinnamon, fresh citrus, coffee, onions, and smoked meat, immediately elevated Drew's mood. For the first time in days, he finally felt some sense of peace.

Several other survivors, Jeff, Julie, Rose, Eileen, Sergeant Bill, and an older gentleman Drew had yet to meet were already seated at a long benched table in the center of the room. Three others Drew was unacquainted with stood against the wall, foraging heads down in tin cups full of stew; two guys in their mid-thirties and a striking black gent in his late twenties, all in uniform and all filthy. They looked up at Drew with curiosity when the three men entered the room.

Shark irreverently took a seat while Major Nate strode over and threw a log on the fire.

"For those of you who have not met him yet, this is Drew McFarland. May you accept him into this community of ours graciously," Major Nate instructed.

"Well, speaking of grace, one of you boys better shut that door cause it's getting cold in here," a light skinned black woman said, emerging from a dark corner of the room with a tray of fresh biscuits. She was very attractive and in her late twenties from what Drew could tell.

"Crystal, what do you know about the cold? You never been outa Flarida," the heavy set woman blurted out, teasing in a strong Jersey accent.

"Well Martha, I can tell you it don't take traveling around the country in an RV to know Florida is pronounced with an O not an A, and you don't know shit about Brunswick stew," Crystal responded. She looked at Drew and nodded a nice to meet you over the steaming tray. "This crazy old Jewish chick is trippin', Major."

Martha batted the statement out of the air with a wave of her hand then offered it to Drew.

"Martha Appleman, I heard alls aboutcha, Drew. About how you and Shark here rescued Elizabeth and Jeff off the top of the Hampton Inn. Pretty heroic I would say. Make yourself at home and get something to eat."

Shark punched Drew playfully in the side and smiled, "Hear that, hero? Already making a name for yourself."

The three men against the wall snorted and chuckled to see the new guy ribbed and made their introductions as well.

The black fellow was Daryl Stephenson, a senior athlete at the University of North Florida in Jacksonville, a baseball player. He had clearly chummed up with Shark over the past couple of days and when the Shark wasn't looking over at Elizabeth, he was exchanging devilish glances with him.

It didn't take long to realize Crystal was Daryl's girlfriend. She was an island native with a high school education and grew up around her father's seafood restaurant. She was next in line to her father's throne and clearly knew what she was doing in the kitchen.

The two others against the wall were Jason Freeman and Buddy Parker.

Jason was a quiet multitalented tradesman, a hayseed of a guy, wiry with greasy brown hair and farm-hand-strong. He had been a part of the Major's original "band of brothers." Now he was in charge of the blacksmith shop and worked on projects with Max.

"A craftsman and jack of all trades," Major Nate said.

Buddy Parker had been the shooter when they first secured the fort and the ultimate savior of life here. His concealed carry permit didn't allow him to bring a weapon into Fort Clinch State park but clearly this ox of a guy followed a less complex set of rules. Fun loving and a simple man, he was a Georgia good ole boy and had just been down camping and fishing by himself as he recovered from a divorce. He now wore a uniform as well.

"I fill it out nicely, don't you think?" he said, shaking Drew's hand.

Drew noticed the Park Service didn't have any problem with Buddy carrying his Glock 27 anymore. This time it was worn on the outside, on his hip.

Drew ate at the table next to Sam Appleman, the older gentleman in his mid-sixties, a Jersey lawyer. He had been a powerful man in the Atlantic City courtroom at one time but henpecked and showing signs of post traumatic stress disorder from his life at home with Martha. His wife had allowed him to buy the motorhome and head south. That had probably been what saved his heart.

"I came down here to get away from Martha's family, only to find the whole world had turned into carnivorous beasts. I could have saved 276 thousand bucks by staying home with those carnivorous beasts," Sam said.

"I'm hearing everything ya sayin'," Martha threatened.

Sam pretty much stayed in the kitchen and helped with prep work as Martha seemed to have a pretty tight leash on him.

Drew was halfway through his tin bowl of the wonderful chowder when the door opened and Bella rushed in. Josh was at the doorway and pushed the Colonel over the threshold.

"At ease ladies and gentlemen," the old man belted out. "Buddy and Jason, you guys are up next on the wall. Shark and Daryl, if you don't mind relieving Max and Carey for a bit, I'm sure they wouldn't mind eating."

Shark gulped down the last of his stew, grabbed two biscuits and headed with Daryl out the door when the Colonel wheeled himself over beside Drew and put out his hand.

"Sorry we have not met yet, Colonel Wilcox, commander here at Fort Clinch."

"Only in title," Crystal teased.

Colonel Wilcox cut his eyes at Crystal playfully and then over to Major Nate who pretended not to hear but poked senselessly at the fire.

Drew could tell this was a good man but black and white with no grey in between. A true Colonel from Vietnam, he had lost his leg in battle and his army had soon lost its interest in him. His only command for the past forty years had been a ragtag group of reinactors working the daily operations of the fort he was a full time resident of. He knew the place inside and out.

Drew could tell those around him had quickly grown to love and respect the man in a very short time and felt that an interesting dynamic had taken place here. The man in the wheelchair and the man still poking at the fire were the real deal, leaders. The dried up tumbleweed they had been in the previous world had taken root in this new one and they had taken control. The place wasn't perfect but in just mere days these gentlemen had taken very strong personalities and were constructing a working machine out of them. The beauty of it all was those they led didn't seem to notice they were all following suit. It was all working naturally.

After they ate, Colonel Wilcox and Major Nate had Drew, Elizabeth, and Jeff stay behind. Nate brought out a map of the fort (a trifold brochure from the gift shop) and laid it out on the table. Drew took a photo of it with his iPhone as Colonel Wilcox pointed out the locations of the various buildings that skirted the parade ground as well as where all of the facilities were.

"What I want to go over with the three of you is what we have planned in case of a breach."

Elizabeth looked alarmed.

The Colonel continued, "Here, we have five separate bastions, each with a narrow spiral staircase leading to the top. Each bastion is accessed via its own tunnel from the parade grounds, like spokes on a wheel. If there is a breach, the alarm will sound and everyone has been instructed to move to the closest bastion in range. Jason has been in the blacksmith shop working on a way to block the staircases once you reach the top. From these vantage points we have a clear view of the entire structure. It would be our only fighting chance and right now we are working on having stockpiles of food, water, and weapons at each of the bastions along with plenty of ammunition.

"So, who will sound this alarm?," Jeff asked.

"Rose," Major Nate said. "She is to ring bell from up in the infirmary. We are certainly concerned about her safety, so Max and Jason have reconfigured the external staircases with pins so that when they are pulled, they will fall away from the building. That leaves the top floor inaccessible. In theory, if all works out, we should have the advantage of all the high ground, be able to squelch the breach, and retake control of the structure. I want to say ladies and gentlemen, a modern military establishment with all of its miles of chain link fence and barbwire has now moved into the obsolete category. This old place was built for this type of conflict. We should be quite safe here," the Major said, injecting the last bit after noticing Elizabeth's concern. "Once we can get that swing-bridge up, we will be sealed in completely and we will be able to relieve some of the burden of watching the gate all the time." He continued, "I have been working with Max on a solution and we should have it up soon. For right now though it remains our Achilles heel."

"There was already an incident there I've been told?" Drew asked.

Major Nate looked at the Colonel and let him speak.

"An idea had been raised to capture a Drinker in order to study their behavior. It was a man named Billy Jameson who made the argument for it, but it was rejected because of the danger involved.

Billy was not fond of the decision the group made

against it so when he was on duty one night, he and another guard named David Howard, brought one of them in and put the entire place at risk. Somehow, they were able to loosen the chains on the gate and got it through without incident until they brought it into the guardroom. Fortunately, they were able to shut and lock the door from inside the building before it broke from its tether and attacked them. The rest of the shift the gate remained unmanned," Colonel Wilcox said.

"Yeah, and it's been hard to sleep since then, Colonel," Crystal commented, pouring all of them a fresh cup of coffee.

"Jesus," Elizabeth said. "What happened after that?"

"Well, there are individual prison cells in the guardroom and we were able to contain the Drinker in one and Billy in another. David did not survive," The Major explained.

"So Billy is now a prisoner?" Drew asked.

"No, Billy is one of the Walkers, if that is what you want to call them," The Colonel said.

"And what is your plan with them?" Elizabeth said, raising the concern in her voice.

The Colonel replied, staring down in his mug, "Just as Billy had originally suggested, we are starving them."

That night, Drew tried not to let his insomnia disturb the others who were passed out in their bunks around him.

Bella, who had started out curled up at his feet, had finally given up with all his tossing and turning, whined, and skittered off to lay by the fireplace hearth that warmed the room of the enlisted men's barracks.

That had been over an hour ago. It was his first night

on dry land in days and the lumpy, pine straw filled mattress (stained with god only knows what from all the tourists over the years), dug its bulges into his back.

He felt like puking.

The room was rocking, as if he were still at sea. Like a drunk recovering from a painful binge, he had one foot on the floor to ease the phantom motion while the events of the day, the previous couple of days, continued to reel out in his mind like an animated flip book.

He dwelled on his decision to stay, it had been instinctual. He had so quickly chosen to bond with this amalgam of survivors in a cold stark fort in Northeast Florida without knowing all of the other options and he was now feeling a sense of depression and failure. He thought of his yacht out alone and exposed in the darkness and pictured Hannah and Cole's names painted across the stern. Drew felt like he had abandoned them that afternoon when he set foot into Shark's RIB and they sped away. It was just a stupid boat but it represented something more, his direction in life. The world was always getting in the way of his plans, and once again, he had been knocked into a sea of ferocious currents and tremendous waves that carried him away. He was tumbling in the whitewater, drowning, and resigning.

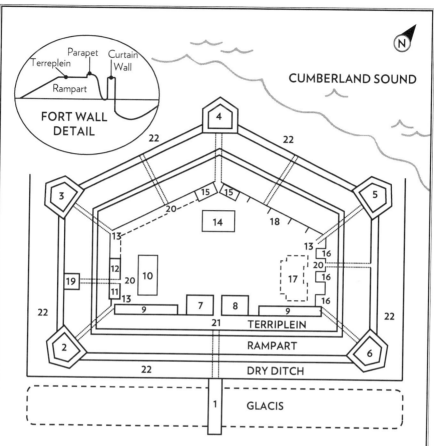

CUMBERLAND SOUND

FORT CLINCH

1. Swing Bridge (Pivots at middle)
2. South Bastion (One of five defensive forts outside the fort)
3. Southwest Bastion
4. Northwest Bastion
5. North Bastion (Mounted Howitzers to fire canister along walls)
6. East Bastion
7. Prison
8. Gaurd Rooms
9. Ramps (Access to top of walls)
10. Enlisted Men's Barracks
11. Bakery (Huge ovens for baking)
12. Blacksmith Shop
13. Bastion Galleries (Bastion tunnels)
14. Storehouse/Sundries (Hospital above, Quartermaster & Sutler below)
15. Lumber Shed
16. Kitchens/Laundry
17. Unfinished Officer's Quarters
18. Prados (Unfinished barracks)
19. Enlisted Men's Latrine
20. Curtain Wall Galleries (Access to outer walls)
21. Sallie Port (Fort Entrance/Exit)
22. Curtain Wall/Scarps (Outer wall/ dry ditch)

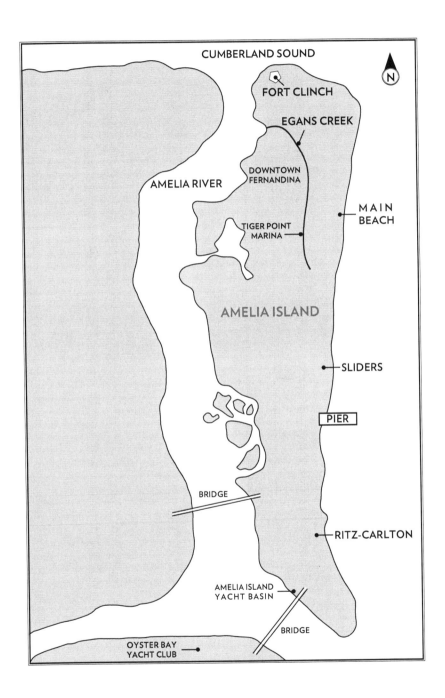

Chapter 12

Drew was stirred awake hours later. It started with heavy panting in his ear. He readjusted in his sleep but the rapid breathing persisted.

A cold, fleshy tongue dragged across his cheek.

He opened his eyes to find Bella being held down from the top bunk by Shark.

"Nice to see that your up, Drew. Spoke with the Major Nate this morning. Told him I picked you for my team," Shark said.

"Yeah, you are in for a real treat with this one," Daryl said from across the row of bunks.

He was leaning forward, looking at his reflection in a shabby full length mirror on the wall, inspecting his immaculate teeth.

Shark ignored him and held out one of the blue wool Union uniforms with striped pants.

"Here, put these on, it's cold outside," he instructed.

Drew noted the stripes on the sleeve. Same rank as he had been by the time he departed the Air Force, Sergeant, and meaningless now.

He put on the uniform and strapped the .45 around his waist.

"After breakfast, D and I will show you around. We got a shopping list to make," Shark said.

Shark led the long blue line of three out the door of the barracks and across the parade ground to the kitchen. The skies were graying and seagulls were circling, preparing for their own breakfast just over the wall. The air was heavy but brought no rain and fog hung low over the ground. From a distance, you wouldn't be able to tell the Union staff sergeant in the middle was wearing 2013 Sperry sail-tech shoes.

Bella disappeared in the haze altogether.

After a breakfast of smoked ham and biscuits and getting Crystal's list of needs, Shark's "team" had made their rounds and it did not take long for Drew to familiarize himself with the layout of the fort. It was comforting to see that the park service had literally kept it running as it had been in the late 19th century. That meant they had a fully functioning blacksmith shop (Jason Freeman's new realm), the bakery (now converted to a shower area), the infirmary, and below it, a sundries shop with a whole slew of uniforms, supplies, and hardware that could be used as primitive weapons.

The problem Drew could clearly see was they would eventually need much more to survive a long haul. The onboard supplies wouldn't last even this small group but couple of weeks, at most. The steady flow of fresh water was a lifesaver but food was at an emergent level as were weapons and ammunition. Overall, they could do with anything they could come by.

Concluding the tour, they ended up at the front entrance to the fort. A set of keys hung on a hook just outside the door of a small brick building to the right of the front sally port.

As the trio approached, Drew noticed iron bars bolted into all of its window frames. It was the only building on the grounds that had them other than the blacksmith shop.

The commotion from inside began the minute Shark turned one of the keys into the lock of the building's massive oak door.

"You fellas go on ahead, I'll wait out here. Crystal would be pissed if she found out I puked up her famous biscuits," Daryl said, as Drew and Shark crossed the threshold.

Drew understood Daryl's concern the moment he entered, the smell.

The stark room contained a single set of bunks, a simple wooden rifle rack and small desk in the center of the room. The floor was remarkably worn, its herringbone pattern of bricks appeared as if they had been in direct weather. The brick walls had seen a plaster covering at one time, but had come down in sheets, exposing the bare brick beneath their crumbling skin. Three cells faced inward to the room. The two to the east held infected neighbors and the one to the west remained empty but for a single cot and empty shackles that lay about the floor.

Drew was comforted to see that the Drinker's cell held a massive wooden door with a small barred window. "1890's style solitary confinement," he said under his breath, as a female drinker smashed her mouth against the iron bars of the small window.

Drew involuntarily reared back as she lashed her tongue out of her mouth, scraping it bloody on splintered teeth, ruined from constant impact with the bars.

"Croaaaat, Croaaaat," she belched out, as she appeared to try and pry the iron rods of the window apart with her face.

"Meet Heidi. You can't see her uniform but she is in hospital scrubs. A nurse maybe," Shark said.

"Must have made her morning tea with water from the river of Lethe," Drew said.

"What's that?" Shark asked.

"Never mind,"

The neighboring cell was blocked by a full length barred door bolted firmly into a solid frame. Behind it was Billy Jameson. Billy was in his filthy corporal's uniform and smelled horrendous. Drew could see oily stains blossoming under his armpits and down around his crotch area. His period brogans were smudged in shit that had run down his pant legs and the leather looked sodden from fluid seeping out of his lower extremities. The thick wool uniform had clearly protected his limbs and torso from any skin puncturing bite marks, another good reason to be suited up in these new duds, Drew took mental note of.

At first, Drew could not see any apparent injuries but then Billy's neck made a crunching sound like car tires on a gravel road as he turned his head exchanging focus between Drew and Shark. His head listed off slightly to one side as his sea glass eyes gazed expressionless upon the potential food sources.

"Probably broke it from getting hit from behind while

trying to run away, the fucking coward. Douche bag almost got us all killed." Shark leaned in closer to the arms held out from between the bars. Billy's finger tips were almost touching Shark's nose. "He also has a bitemark you can't see on the back of his head. It is nasty; you can see his bare fucking dome."

"So, the plan is to starve them?" Drew asked, switching subjects.

"Major was against it at first, but agreed that we need to learn what we can from them. The hope is that Billy and his girlfriend here will peter out and fade away without any din-din after time," Shark replied.

"Well, the food source doesn't just include humans from what I saw on the beach at Cumberland," Drew pointed out. "They were able to take down a horse."

"Yeah but there are no horses here, and once they run out of people, pets, and pigeons, I imagine that they won't be able to survive through the Florida summer. Right now, it is pretty cold but I imagine shitbag here would be a lot worse off it were 100 degrees. I'm not looking forward to that 'cause as it is now, Febreeze wouldn't cover up the stink that's in here. Can't imagine what it will be like in a week, or month from now." Shark paused, "It's been days now though and these guys haven't seemed to slow all that much. They don't sleep, they don't eat, they just mill in their cells, anxious to glimpse at their next meal. It is interesting though, that they seem to be oblivious of each other. It is just when there is fresh meat around that they start getting really agitated."

"Well. Their possible demise may mean there is light at the end of the tunnel," Drew responded.

"One can hope," Shark said.

"Are you guys done bullshitting in there, I am freezing

my black ass off out here," Daryl called from outside.

"Hey Daryl, Quit yer bitching, and by the way you aren't black, you're red-boned," Shark chided.

It was just after noon and once again, they found themselves back in Crystal's kitchen. The fireplace inside was alive and there were beautiful whiting that Martha was spinning on a rotisserie. The smell was incredible.

Crystal refilled coffee while Drew, Shark, Daryl, Sergeant Bill, and Major Nate gathered around a large map of Amelia Island that he had spread out on the table.

Drew could see that Amelia resembled the body of a grasshopper, sans the legs. It was approximately 13 miles long and 4 miles wide at its widest point. There were two bridges that served as the only access points; one approximately in the middle of the island that crossed to the mainland and one at the southern tip that crossed over to Big Talbot Island, another state park.

The Major pointed out the housing, hotels, and resort areas that ran along the Atlantic side and the commercial areas along the Intracoastal Waterway–all potential areas to gain supplies. Right now, they were assessing the risks involved with each but they agreed they would first need a new boat. The small RIB from Shark's *Minerva* just was not going to be sufficient for any major hauls.

"Just to the north of the city, there is a small creek that leads to a full service marina. That may be your best bet. It has never been a very populated area to begin with and I know there is a high barb wire fence that surrounds it," Major Nate said.

"You are just going to have to see for yourselves. The place could be swarming for all I know."

"I can tell you I like it because it seems to be pretty close by. If that marina is secure, I would like to tie up my boat there and get her off of that exposed mooring. I have a number of supplies and food aboard that we could use as well," Drew offered.

"We will leave tomorrow, bright and early then. Sounds like dinner is on you, tomorrow night," Shark winked.

"Hope you like MREs," Drew said.

"Well with no cooking involved, that will free up Crystal to watch the front gate," Bill teased.

Crystal glared at him, "the shit if I will."

They continued to laugh throughout lunch. Conversation, warm fish and southern potato cakes certainly helped to make everything feel alright, despite being surrounded by death. Nearly the whole crew of survivors had filled the room once again (all but Shark and Daryl who had taken over their turn at the gate). As they told their stories Drew could feel the group of survivors growing tighter. They were getting back something now, a chance. Not just an opportunity at survival but an opportunity to have fellowship. Looking around the room Drew felt that it was probably just as important as food and water. Somehow he was beginning to appreciate these strange people. They were all he had.

"Anyone here other than my troops ever shoot a musket before?" Major Nate asked the group. He had lightened up after a few drinks and led the party outside.

✛ ✛ ✛

It was late afternoon and the sun was going down as Drew lay in his bunk and looked out the window of his room in the barracks. He could see the silhouette of the Major and Rose high up on the wall. Every minute or so a shot would ring out and Bella, curled at Drew's feet, would flinch. Everyone had taken their turn and had gone about their business but Rose especially had taken keen interest in the dated weapon and persisted. Drew had seen it on her face the first time she pulled the trigger, the surprise, the power, the release. She was hooked.

They had been firing at the Drinkers, leaving the slower, rotting dead alone for the most part. The Drinkers were the real problem Major Nate believed (as did Drew). It was their speed, intensity, and awareness that was the threat. There was power and strength behind them and a certain ferocity that was lacking in their slower counterparts.

Chapter 13

The Atlantic Ocean was extremely calm the next morning as Shark, Daryl, and Drew cut across its surface in the small RIB. It was still dark and overcast and the temperature felt Arctic as the open aired boat picked up speed and headed around the tip of Amelia Island in the direction of downtown Fernandina.

To their left, Drew could make out several steel buildings he recalled from the map. They were next to two large tubular silos with a long elevator that fed the top of the towering structures with sawdust–a cardboard mill, as Major Nate had pointed out on the map. This marked the mouth of Egan's Creek, the waterway to their destination marina.

As Shark hugged closer to shore and they were able to get a better look at the massive structures off to port. It appeared quiet.

Just ahead, there was an open area with a bombed out early 80's GMC stake bed, rusting amongst a pile of scrap and an enormously fat drinker in tattered overalls that was standing on one of the stubby piers that jutted out into the waterway.

The Drinker had run out to greet them and was too out of breath to make the usual croaking sound. Nearly 20 feet from them, he just panted and glared. His fists clenched open and closed as they continued on.

"That juice just ain't worth the squeeze," Daryl commented.

"Roger that," Shark replied as he pressed the RIB into the mouth of Egan's Creek.

It was getting lighter now and as they rounded the bend, Drew was relieved to see *Hannah* off toward the city, still at her mooring, quiet in the distance.

Up ahead to starboard, Drew could see the first of the Tiger Point Marina's five T-docks that ran parallel to the waterway. To port, there was nothing but marsh land that terminated into a wooded tree line far off in the distance.

At the end of the first T-dock, there was a large Schooner showing nothing but masts above the waterline. Her mass had drug down the end of the wooden pier with it and caused the small fishing boat across from to her to go under, stern first. Its bow jutted up from the water.

The whole pier looked precarious so they continued on, keeping an eye on the other two sailboats tied there. They scanned for movement and it was all clear. The gangway that led to it was quiet as well, all the way up to the street. This looked promising.

Their small craft approached the next T dock. It was a longer floating dock where four newer sailboats were berthed, all Catalina 25s with vinyl decals on their sides denoting the Amelia Sailing School.

Nearby, a pontoon houseboat converted into a party barge had *The Palace II* written in messy, hand painted letters across its stern. It took the far inside of the pier and Drew scoped out a space across from it where he could berth *Hannah*. From shore, the bombed out floating bar could block view of *Hannah* to some extent. As well, this dock was connected to the mainland by an aluminum gangway that raised and lowered as the tide changed. It was pinned at the pivot point and would be easy to release and drop away into the water, blocking access to the pier by about 30 feet.

Two Walkers began down the gangway from the parking lot above. One was a scarecrow of a man in coveralls stained with blood and covered in what most likely was the white powder of fiberglass dust. The other was perhaps one of the sailing school's instructors. His starched navy blue button down shirt had Amelia Sailing stitched across the breast pocket of a shirt that was still tucked into his khaki pants. For a couple hundred dollars, rich guys would pay to have these guys take them offshore and snap pictures of them at the helm. Pictures that would ultimately sit on an office shelf somewhere, lying about what a big worldly badass the guy behind the desk was.

"Pull alongside here," Drew guided Shark at the helm.

The RIB pulled along the empty space on the pier and Daryl stepped immediately off of the boat, followed by Drew.

They looked warily at the party barge, Drew with his .45 drawn and Daryl with a shotgun. They couldn't see into the dingy windows and were not in the mood for any ambush.

Quickly, they moved around and approached their aggressors.

Not wanting to fire any rounds, Daryl met the first, thin, dusty Walker and had him over the railing and in the water in seconds with the butt of the shotgun.

Drew was on Mr. Preppy.

Meeting him halfway up the gangplank Drew crouched low, rushed, and hoisted the sailing school rep over the aluminum railing into the water. The man immediately sank out of sight.

It took a bit of a struggle getting the oxidized pins out of the gangway on the mainland side but Drew managed and it finally splashed into the water.

Shark brought the RIB around, picked up Drew and brought him back over to the isolated pier.

There hadn't turned out to be much aboard the factory stark sailing school Catalina's other than six handheld marine radios that they were able to pick up, as well a couple bags of potato chips. Shark investigated the *Palace II* and was pleased to find a stockpile of liquor and warm beer aboard. He also recovered a costume pirate's hat and eye patch that he promptly put on.

"Man you look like you got an identity crisis," Daryl said. He looked over at Drew, "Nigga don't know if he is Blackbeard or General Sherman."

Shark winked with his uncovered eye and took a hard pull on a bottle of Malibu.

The three of them climbed to the rooftop deck of the *Palace II*. From this perspective, it was clear that this area had not been very populated to begin with and didn't have much of a draw (not if you were one of the infected, that is).

Shark pointed to the marina. There was a high chain length fence that ran around the entire property all the way to the water line. A large steel building and a couple worn outbuildings made up the Egan's creek marina property. A number of sailboats in various stages of repair lay quiet and still on the hard in the lot beside a main office. Drew saw movement and noticed a handful of Walkers milling around outside of the fence but other than that, things looked relatively inactive.

"Let's do this," Shark said, giving the green light.

The Tiger Point Marina had a main boat ramp that was flanked on either side by two short piers. As the RIB approached around the first pier to the right of the ramp, they saw the marina's infected.

They surrounded a massive sailboat, the *Jolly Mon*, held high in the air by a wheeled boat lift. It appeared that they had spent days scratching at the hull's antifouling paint which was now worn to bare fiberglass in many places.

The dead were so distracted by the *Jolly Mon* that they did not notice the sound of the approaching outboard until the trio had already tied off to a broken piling 10 yards out from the ramp.

"Fellas, watch for the Drinkers." Drew said, heart pounding in his chest.

Just then, they heard the sound of batter boards being removed from the *Jolly Mon's* companionway.

A salty looking middle aged man with warn denim jeans and a bright red sweater appeared in the cockpit of the vessel. He was holding a steaming mug of coffee.

"If you gentlemen stay tied up there I am gonna have to charge you fifteen dollars a day," he called out, raising his mug.

The infected were now in hysteria over his sudden appearance but had also now taken notice of the new meal plan that just arrived by boat. Drew counted three Drinkers and seven Walkers that surrounded the boat. From the looks of it they must have been the only infected that were inside the fence. They were almost comical in their indecision on which target to focus on.

Without conference, shots broke the silence as Shark took aim with the AR and began taking them out. Within seconds, they all lay silent on the ground around the suspended yacht.

Shark lowered the rifle.

"Well, I guess that's that," Drew said and climbed cautiously up onto the pier, followed by Daryl and Shark.

"Thanks for your help gentlemen, I was just about to run out of groceries," The man said, climbing down from the swim ladder. "Name is Tom White, I'm the harbormaster here, or at least was," he said, looking at the recently silenced infected at his feet. He held out his hand. "Would introduce you to the rest of my staff but as you can see they are preoccupied."

"Shit Tom, you been up there all this time?" Drew asked, returning the man's firm, leathery handshake.

"I was working an electrical problem in that old tub when the shit hit the fan and I been aboard ever since. Probably fortunate for me that Jimmy here was able to shut the gate before he became one of them," he said and nudged the shoulder of a rotting corpse with the toe of his Timberland's.

Drew looked toward the chain length gate that was slowly beginning to crowd with Walkers. Several others were meandering down the main road toward the marina now, clearly drawn by the sound of the gunfire.

"How secure is this place?" Drew asked.

"Safe as it looks. I imagine if there were more of them they may be able to come through the fence, but for now, I don't believe that we should have any surprises," Tom said. Looking at the bodies around him, he continued, "Taking roll here I you believe got every one of them. Thanks again for your help."

Shark nodded indifferently and scanned the area again for movement.

"You guys mind explaining the getup?" Tom asked.

Drew was confused by the question at first but quickly realized how their group must look with the three of them in uniform. Shark still had the pirate hat on, his eye patch now on his forehead, shifted out of the way from when he used the rifle.

They briefly explained their situation at Fort Clinch to Tom and he more than agreed to tag along.

"Anything I can do to help," Tom offered. "Now that boat you are after, I think I have just what you guys are looking for."

Daryl headed over to patrol the fence line while Tom led Shark and Drew over to a large steel building beside the marina office. Inside, a brand new Grady White Canyon 306 center console fishing boat lay nestled on her trailer. Its custom deep black hull looked as if it had never seen a single UV ray. Two mercury outboards hung from the transom just beside the words, *Twist of Fate* painted in silver lettering on her rear quarters.

"The owner, a real cocksucker, he buys a hundred and fifty thousand dollar fishing boat, no problem. But then he wants to argue about paying our storage fee. We have been holding onto it until he coughs up the cash," Tom said, lowering the trailer onto the ball hitch of a boat tractor. "I got the keys in the office and I can have her splashed in minutes. We are a full service marina here and my fuel tanks were topped off just days before this thing hit. We should be all set on diesel and marine gas for some time-as long as the marina stays clear of those things."

Tom was right, within the half hour, the Mercurys roared to life and the four men were aboard the *Twist of Fate*. They had combed the marina of supplies, tools, and food from the marina office and the various boats that peppered the area. Daryl had even come up with a tired .38 and two boxes of ammunition from the glove compartment of an old Ford Taurus station wagon that had belonged to a marina staff member. Drew found several cases of Stabile fuel stabilizer and had the idea of pouring some into the holding tanks of a number of the boats in the yard. Who knew how long the fuel would be good for as time wore on? The stabilizer should buy them some time.

With the RIB in tow, they headed out of the marina, under a small bridge, and continued deeper into the throat of Egan's creek. The marsh continued on to port as rows of private residences appeared to starboard, their long docks reaching to the water.

Drew felt as if he was having déjà vu.

Oh god, this again, he thought to himself, even though he had agreed this area was perhaps their safest bet for supplies. Nevertheless, he had already experienced the dangers a place like one of these houses could hide.

They passed by several private docks before deciding upon one that seemed more remote from the rest. The plan was to anchor the *Twist* just offshore and use the much more maneuverable RIB for ferrying to and from the pier.

Tom stayed back with the *Twist* while Drew, Shark, and Daryl stepped off the RIB onto the weathered planks of the pier.

Drew imagined a pack of Drinkers scampering down the dock toward them but none came.

"Jesus, this is crazy," Daryl said.

"Probably should have seen some of them already with the sound of the Merc's," Shark tried to reassure the others. "It looks quiet," he continued, lowering his AR as if comfortable with the situation, Mr. Cool.

They continued up the long length of pier to a large two story Ranch style house with sliding glass doors that opened out onto a wooden deck. There was an open Weber grill with an unrecognizable meat that had transformed into coal while the propane ran out. A beer bottle and a glass of wine stood on a picnic table, rainwater having filled them, their contents had diluted to a hazy pale yellow murk.

Approaching slowly, Drew tried the handle on the sliding door. It slid back an inch, gently in its tracks. He was almost disappointed to see that it was unlocked.

"I'm telling you guys, this is stupid." Daryl protested. He obviously was sharing some of the same emotions that Drew was feeling about the situation.

"Would you rather head downtown? Maybe get valet parking and pick up takeout for every one?" Shark whispered in frustration. His nerves were up as well.

"Shit man, I'm just saying," Daryl replied.

Before any more protest, Shark slid through the door and into the dark kitchen, weapon ready.

Daryl rolled his eyes at Drew and motioned for him to follow. The three paused just inside the doorway, standing in silence, listening for any sign of disturbance. The only sound in the house was a single beep every several minutes from a smoke detector that complained of a dead battery.

Staying together, they quickly moved through the house. The first thing that they noticed was that the front door was shut and locked, very strange-was someone still here?

"Anyone home?" Drew called, out breaking the silence and then bracing for some unknown impact. There was nothing. Perhaps they left by boat.

Shark drew back the curtains covering a window next

to the front door. They stared out across an open front yard to a group of three houses across the street. All was quiet. No infected were to be seen. The only thing out of place was a late model, powder blue BMW sedan parked partially up on the grass in one yard. The driver's side door stood open.

"What the fuck?" Daryl commented. "Looks like the party is already over and I just got here."

Not letting their guard down, they continued through the downstairs.

Simple middle class people had lived here. The owner of the house also appeared to own a local pest control service in town. Pictures on a wall office showed his opening in September, 1986. The reasonably attractive wife looked to be a homemaker, raising two teenage girls. They hadn't had much but what they did have showed pride in ownership. It made Drew feel strangely sad and angry for their loss. This wasn't fair, this whole fucking thing. It was getting old now, time out, game over. He wanted this end but they could only press on room to room.

They moved upstairs in laminar flow. The staircase led to a hallway with four separate bedrooms. These rooms were fruitless, empty, boxes; just reminders of the previous inhabitants.

Continuing down the end of the hall there was a door to a room over the garage.

"Fucking jackpot," Shark said as soon as he swung the door open.

It was nothing short of a man-cave, this guy's getaway was equipped with a large maroon leather pit couch, a 65 inch LED TV, movie posters on the wall, and a huge pool table in the center of the room. Drew was curious as to how they had been able to get it all up there.

"You're not lying, I wonder if this guy's wife has a

sister," Daryl said, rolling the cue ball into a side pocket.

"Dude, I'm not talking about the pool table. Those are gun cabinets against that wall," Shark said and picked up the marine radio.

"Yo Tom, sit tight for a bit, we may have a score here," he said.

Within minutes they had located the gun cabinet keys in a desk drawer of the man's office downstairs and were now staring at a full arsenal of weapons: 7 rifles, 4 shotguns, 10 pistols and hundreds of rounds of ammunition.

Despite their excitement, the owner had left with nothing and it was strange. Drew imagined the infected pouring into Burt's house and it put him on edge. Suddenly, he wished that they had brought Bella with them as she made a hell of a freak detector, but Josh had asked that she stay behind to play.

"Let's just pack these up and get the fuck out of here. I don't like the feel of this," he suggested.

"You don't have to tell me twice," Daryl said.

Just then the radio cracked alive at Sharks hip, "Fellas, you're going to have company in t-minus 5 seconds. Two girls, running fast and coming around the side of the house…"

Downstairs, the sound of plate glass shattering across the tile kitchen floor tore through the silence of the house. Daryl slammed the door of the man cave shut as Drew and Shark fought with a section of the leather couch to block it with.

They were out of time. They could hear the thuds of scrambling footfall coming up the stairs then down the hall. It grew louder as the thin hollow door splintered inward upon the girls' impact with it. A second strike tore the door completely out of the framework.

Two frantic teenagers of about 13 and 16 stood panting

in the room. They selected targets and went for them.

Daryl immediately lunged backward and without hesitation put a 12 gauge round through the younger girl's chest as she dove for him.

Torn nearly in half, she fell to the floor in a heap.

Shark was able to spin and avoid the lunge of the older one but just narrowly.

Drew dropped to his knees, steadied his .45 on the back of the leather sofa and put a round through her head.

Suddenly, the younger girl's upper half twitched back into action and her head began snapping with lifeless jaws. Attempting to ambulate forward toward Daryl again, she dug her fingernails into the hardwood, leaving white claw marks as they tore through the finish.

Shark swung his rifle and crushed her smacking skull.

The three of them stood together trying to recapture their breath and gather their wits about them.

"Gentlemen, what's your status? I repeat, what is your status? Over," Tom came across frantic on the radio, jerking the room back into focus.

"We were able to take them out," Shark spoke back calmly, "headed down now and ready to call it a day, over."

"I'm sorry, I don't know what happened guys. They came from out of nowhere. I would have warned you sooner, over," Tom said.

The group found a large duffel bag and moved fast gathering the up the weapons and ammunition and taking it all down to the porch at the rear of the house. Once again, they were on high alert as they circled around to each side of the residence. Strangely enough, both side gates were still firmly shut and locked.

"What the fuck?" Shark said.

"Fellas, come check this out." Daryl said, looking down at a break in the lattice that covered the crawlspace under the house. "It looks like this was where they were hiding."

Drew knelt and lit the darkness with his penlight, quickly discovering where the parents of the two girls had gone.

They had not made it out by boat but had been drug under the house to be consumed by the two fiends. Gnawed body parts were strew across the sandy ground, discarded alongside empty paint cans and scrap lumber. He imagined that the family pet must also be down there somewhere.

"Like fucking alligators on the Discovery channel, dragging their prey under logs to dine on later," Shark commented.

With that, Daryl lost his girlfriend's biscuits.

While Daryl was getting his composure back, Drew and Shark picked up the pace and made several trips back and forth to the house loading up the RIB with supplies, batteries, flashlights, and some blankets they had scavenged from the upstairs bedrooms. The kitchen had turned out to offer a nice stockpile of canned goods, pastas, and miscellany, and there was a large bowl of apples on the counter top that had not yet turned.

The weapons remained to be the largest score on this run. Drew also made a trip to the garage and splashed some fuel stabilizer into the tanks of the two family vehicles, a modest Honda accord and a large black Suburban.

Within thirty minutes they were back aboard the *Twist*, headed back toward the mouth of Egan's Creek and then south toward the *Hannah Cole*.

Hannah's waterline rose dramatically as Drew and Daryl unloaded her supplies into the *Twist*. Drew felt comfortable now that she was double tied with shock lines to the pier they had isolated earlier, but there was an underlying anger brewing within him. Looking upon the provisions that he had taken so many months to calculate, now being unpacked from his lovely boat, he felt himself again resenting the whole situation.

Several Walkers had been attracted to the rumble of the *Fate*'s Mercs and ambled down what was left of the walkway–stopping short, unable to reach their prey.

"Mother fuckers," Drew said, raising his pistol. He fired round at a man in a dirty safety vest and hardhat, perhaps a worker from the nearby cardboard factory. Drew missed the intended target of the man's head. The round passed through his Adam's apple, dead center, and his head flopped back as if on a hinge. He fell forward into the swirling currents of Egan's Creek and quickly disappeared.

"Save your rounds," Shark reminded him.

"Whatever man," Drew said under his breath.

Before their departure, Drew checked over his vessel again. He located a scrap of discarded aluminum siding from the *Palace II* and with a red sharpie he wrote, "Danger, dead inside," and hung it on his locked companionway. It was the only security system he had.

The sky had puckered and it began to rain as the *Twist*

headed back out into the Amelia sound. Shark had taken the wheel and was blaring the Gypsy King's "Bambaleo" over the boat's Bluetooth from his iPhone as they raced at breakneck speed back around the northern end of the island and back to Fort Clinch.

As they approached, Drew looked out at the massive cruise ship beached helplessly on Cumberland. Even in this visibility he could see long brown rust stains that were already beginning to run down the vessel's hull as if she had been weeping from her own demise. Several Walkers were ambling around on the Cumberland south beach after appearing from the woods, clearly drawn by the sound of their new ocean hotrod.

Drew looked away. He was still bitter.

That evening, Major Nate, Shark, Drew, Daryl, and Tom stood around a map of Amelia Island they had pinned to a wall in the enlisted barracks. The Major gave Crystal and Martha the night off and the men were eating out of foil MRE pouches they heated in a pot of boiling water hung from the fireplace spit. It was still cold and rainy outside but everyone was in good spirits.

When they had arrived back at the fort they learned that Max and Jason had been able to secure the drawbridge to the fort. This relieved a lot of the tension permeating the place and allowed the Major to cut down the guards on the gate and those on the wall, down to one per task.

Everyone was also pleased to see a new face. It seemed to add to the feeling of hope that they had already garnered from Max and Jason's success.

Drew certainly thought Tom would prove to be a huge

asset to the group and they were currently discussing his plans to create an electrical grid for the Fort.

"…We need batteries, and lots of them. There are plenty of boats around to secure solar panels and wind vanes. After that, all we need to do is regulate the charge voltage and invert the power. Tapping in directly to the fort's main breakers we should be able to bring this place back to life," Tom said. "If we can score a generator larger than that little Honda we can have a hybrid system with plenty of backup."

"Like a big fucking Prius without the wheels," Shark commented.

"Well…something like that," Tom replied, searching out possible supply zones. "We can go back to my marina and hit the place up again for batteries. We also may have a good chance at the Amelia Yacht Basin," he added, pointing it out on the map. It lay at the foot of the bridge that intersected at the middle of the island. "There is a significant parts inventory warehouse there and scoring some larger AGMs would certainly fit the bill. I will drive tomorrow. Driver always gets the first choice in music," Tom said. He had already begun to take his place within their group.

The room fell silent as shots began to ring out in the distance, one after another, echoing off the walls of the fort. Nobody was alarmed as Rose and Eileen Simmons were up on the wall taking turns with the Remington 770 bolt action .30-06 hunting rifle that their team secured from the man-cave earlier that day. Since the moment the group arrived, the weapon had not left Rose's sight and she carried it around everywhere, slung over her shoulder.

Chapter 14

The next morning the team was off again with Tom at the helm. The sky was clearing and the sun was already trying to burn off the remaining haze, despite the cold.

They would have left earlier, but Jeff had ended up tagging along with them after a long argument with his mom that morning. Elizabeth ended up giving in but insisted that he remain in the boat if the men were to go ashore. Shark had assured her he would hold him to his word and keep him safe. Besides, there were always the radios they each carried, so he would be able to check in with her routinely.

Jeff was a good kid and the whole group respected his desire to participate. Drew watched him as he struggled to give his mom his 30 minute check-in over their roaring engines as they passed once more by the city of Fernandina, off to port. It remained engulfed in a sea of infected who turned their faces toward their boat as they made a pass.

After continuing beyond another large pulp elevator with a number of outbuildings just south of the city, the Intracoastal branched toward the Shave Bridge. When they reached the major thoroughfare, Drew could see the tops of cars lining the entire span in both directions, parked forever. A small inlet paralleled the bridge and a sign on a post delineated the Amelia Island Yacht Basin.

"Slow No Wake," it read.

Just outside the entrance, Tom shut the engines down as Jeff ran to the bow and dropped anchor.

Drew saw from the map that the marina was surrounded on three sides by marsh and was situated north of the bridge alongside highway 200. Isolated as it was, there were still quite a number of boats, six separate docks worth. The compound included two large steel buildings, a restaurant, a marina office, a bathhouse, as well as lots of other places the infected may be hiding.

Drew, Daryl, and Shark approached the first three rows of docks in the RIB. There were a number of large sailboats and several even larger cabin cruisers already showing their need for a good hose down. They perpetually tugged at their restraints in the small wake of the passing dinghy.

"Remind me what we are doing here?" Daryl started in, as that now too familiar feeling of impending doom began to rise up amongst them all.

Everyone remained silent, as they made it all the way to where the marina cut left before they noticed movement. To their port was a narrow peninsula of land that consisted of trailer storage and long term storage that held several boats in dry dock.

Two Walkers, police officers wearing fish and wildlife jackets, caught sight of the RIB and came ambling out from behind one of the box trailers.

Shark sighted-in his AR and was able to have them both on the ground with 5 rounds, but it did not take long for the rifle reports to draw more of them. This time, the infected were beginning to emerge from the two steel buildings that lay (pun intended) dead ahead.

The piers all remained remarkably silent.

"Hey you motherfuckers, over here," Daryl yelled out.

"I don't know which one of you guys is more subtle," Drew said, shaking his head.

Daryl had certainly captured their attention. There appeared to be at least 50 of them as the RIB approached the boat ramp at the foot of the first large steel building. Shark had the RIB just 20 feet from the foot of the ramp but the Walkers that ambled down still would not drive in deeper than their knees.

Lucky for us, Drew thought. "Check it out."

"Yeah, they don't dig the water too much." Daryl said.

"I know, you would think they were black," Shark prodded him.

"Keep on talking, white boy." Daryl returned.

"Guys, that's not what I'm talking about. I'm not seeing any Drinkers," Drew said, picking up his portable radio. "Tom and Jeff, you guys are gonna hear some more gunfire, just letting you know that everything is kosher back here."

With that, they lit the place up, piercing the silence like a grand finale on the Fourth of July. Within two minutes, gun barrels dropped and only the moans of strained boat fenders and sounds of clanking rigging filled the air.

Motionless Walkers lay strewn across the boat ramp and decorated the lot that ran its length to the main office off to the right.

They sat still, every slight movement in the boat making rings that radiated out and bobbed the floating dead at the foot of the ramp.

Still, there were no Drinkers. They let minutes go by and

everything seemed to be all clear.

"Tom, Jeff, we are making landfall, over." Shark spoke into the radio.

"Roger that," Jeff came across. "And Mom just radioed and says there is a large sailboat that looks like it is coming in from offshore, over."

Shark shot a glance at Drew and Daryl. "Ten-four," he radioed back.

To avoid being possibly ambushed, Drew tied the painter of the RIB to a half sunken runabout, just off the peninsula. Weapons drawn, they made their sweep, inspecting the boats on the hard and continuing on to the first steel building. As they made their way inside, stacked high on either side was an array of small power boats and a boat lift that stood dormant off to one side of the room.

"Looks like we may be on to some of those batteries," Shark said, leading them back outside.

The second building was attached to the first by a tall roof section they passed beneath. The open doorway they entered had spilled forth the infected just minutes ago. It turned out to be a large line repair shop with machining capabilities. Small pleasure craft in various states of repair sat on trailers awaiting maintenance. There were large tool chests off to one wall and a row of benches for light work along another. In front of them, several parts shelves towered high in the air. To the right, there was a smaller enclosed room that was marked "Service Office" on a bloodied front door, held on by a single remaining hinge. The room's plate glass windows were smashed and there were clearly signs of a struggle that had taken place inside. Above them, hissing in terror was a black and grey striped cat on the metal roof of the small office.

"Well, that explains why the party was in here," Shark said, leaning a ladder against the side of the enclosure and climbing up.

"Here kitty, kitty," he called, but the cat wasn't having any of it and made its exit via a tower of boxes stacked nearby. "Fucking cat doesn't know what's good for it."

"Shit, I would run from you too," Daryl said.

Shark picked up the radio, "Jeff, don't forget and phone home. It's about that time."

"Yeah sure, how's things your way?" Jeff responded.

"Tom was onto something, it's a fucking jackpot. You guys should be all set to weigh anchor and come on in. We have some loading to do," Shark said, checking out the bottom of one of the long parts shelves.

Brand new, sealed, deep-cycle marine batteries lay two rows deep with the promise of thousands of amp hours worth of juice. The shelf above held voltage regulators with a variety of outputs. There were also 5 wind vanes and 6 large solar panels all new in the box. Spools of marine grade wire, perhaps thousands of feet worth of it, were stacked on a pallet nearby.

"Yup, a fucking jackpot, over," he repeated.

"More marine radios in here," Drew called from the office. I'm counting eight of them and a charging station. Power is off but they are all still fully charged.

"Hey assholes, I hate to one up you but check what I found out back," Daryl said, sticking his head out of a small door at the rear of the building. A huge shit-eating grin was on his face. "It looks to be a diesel generator, says Kobuta 25. It's hardwired directly to the building so I imagine it still works."

Shark's radio cracked to life again. "Ok gents. Looks like you guys made quite a mess out here, over," Tom came across.

Drew peered out the doorway and saw the *Twist*'s black hull pulling alongside the bulkhead just out front.

It took nearly two hours to load all the electrical supplies aboard the boat. Shark hung back with Jeff and helped lift the massive AGM batteries aboard while Tom and Drew disconnected the generator from the building. After a bit of a struggle, it took the jet-ski lift to hoist the massive diesel onto the rear deck of the *Twist of Fate*. While they were working, Daryl had made his way into the parking lot outside the Marina's main office and had been on watch for the infected.

It had been quiet.

Daryl radioed in, "What's the plan?'

"Coming to join you, over," Drew responded, motioning Shark over.

Tom and Jeff were back aboard the *Twist* and guided her back out the entrance of the marina.

The parking lot where Daryl stood was accessed by a road that lead out to State Road 200, the just at the foot of the bridge. As they came closer, they saw that the entrance to the marina had two large tubular steel gates that had been clearly closed and padlocked to block people's ability to exit from the main road or use the property to try and turn around.

Cars were jammed bumper to bumper all along this main artery that accessed the island. It was a total impasse. Steel was clearly so congested here that it would be difficult to make forward progress in any direction without having to travel across the tops of vehicles.

As they approached, there was movement they could see

in a black mini van just outside of the gate. The dark tint on the windows obscured the view until they were closer. Approaching the rear of the Grand Caravan, a sticker on the rear of the vehicle claimed that the man in the driver's seat was a Citadel Alumni. Now, he was just a drinker. Strapped in his seatbelt the man thrashed around as the trio approached.

Shark came along the driver's side door as the man slapped his hands against the window, the gold ring on his hand cracked against the glass. One more strike with it and the window spider webbed into fragments held in place by the tint. The broken glass folded out as the drinker tried to pull himself unsuccessfully through the now open window frame.

Shark reared back and smashed the man's glasses against his face with the butt of his rifle, silencing his awful croaks forever.

The three of them climbed onto the roof of the van and stared out across the traffic jam. There were more of them stuck in their cars all down 200 toward the island and up on the span headed inland. There were also a number of stray Walkers at different locations outside of their vehicles, but they remained boxed in place, a total deadlock.

They hopped down and headed back through the marina entrance, taking a left down a service road to the first three sets of docks. A sign with an arrow pointed, docks A-C, marina restaurant and showers.

The Galley Bar and Grille was a newer looking building, flanked on either side by empty parking lots. A wooden deck that stood off to the left allowed outdoor dining and a view of the entire marina.

Drew climbed the deck's small flight of stairs and entered the bar area where tables and chairs lay on their sides and broken glass littered the floor, crunching under his feet.

The aroma inside emitted from rotten seafood and a single corpse lying face down behind the bar counter in an advancing stage of decomposition. His white chef's blouse had stained through brown and he was greasy with his own ruin.

"Looks like it's an open bar," Shark said, coming up behind Drew."

"Fuck dude, don't do that shit. You scared the crap out of me."

Daryl had already caught a whiff of the chef on his approach and had made an early retreat back out into the parking lot.

"You finding anything Drew?" Shark asked.

"Other than booze I'm not seeing much here," Drew said.

Shark pulled an expensive bottle of Merlot down from a top shelf. "Well, we will just have to salvage what we can," he said with sarcastic apology.

"Hopefully we can salvage your liver," Drew replied, pushing through a swinging door into the small kitchen.

The smell inside the room made it almost hard to breath. Flies buzzed their aerobatic maneuvers ever resituating themselves upon different meals of decay that lay across the countertops. A seagull stood on the side of a sink, pecking at a piece of rotten fish that had been left in mid-filet. The bird didn't seem to mind Drew's presence. It just looked up once with it's empty black eyes and then returned to its meal.

Not expecting much, Drew noticed a deep freezer in the corner and lifted the lid.

"Holy shit. Shark, we need to bring the RIB around."

White vapor poured from the open freezer and swirled at Drew's feet.

"Is that dry ice?" Shark asked in shock, tearing into the find. "And fucking fish?" he dug in deeper, "and fucking shrimp, and fucking burger meat, and fucking steaks, and oh Jesus, lobster fucking tales. Look at all this."

"Like I said, bring the RIB around," Drew said, smiling.

With that, Shark disappeared outside while Drew continued about the room gathering up spices and condiments that he found on various shelves around the room.

Shark and Daryl eventually radioed in and said they found two large, ten day marine coolers in the Marina store and were in the RIB, headed back.

Jeff and Tom were pumped at the news of their discovery as Drew was on the radio explaining their tardiness. He made a mistake assuming that the sound of broken glass under footfall was Shark returning, trying to sneak up on him again. He tried to play along with his back turned to the door when fingers dug a firm grip into his shoulder.

"Fuck man, that hurts," he said, turning.

It was an older, overweight female Walker, her teeth clacking together inches from Drew's face. Her left arm had been chewed away but her right still remained firmly dug into Drew's shoulder. She was still in her red Marina Bar and Grill uniform sweater and Khaki pants. Bird shit had streaked her hair and clothes so thick that it completely blocked out the embroidered logo of the Bar on her breast.

"Oh God," Drew said, falling back between the freezer the wall.

He kicked his feet out and shoved the waitress back briefly, but instantly she was on him again.

Drew fought to remove his pistol from the holster.

She lunged.

Instantly, Shark appeared in the doorway. Grabbing the filet knife, Shark dove forward and slammed it into the back of the monster's head.

Drew saw the blade tip exit the corner of the woman's right eye. The massive weight of her slumped down on top of him. She was dead once again.

"Maybe we shouldn't split up," Shark said, trying to catch his breath.

"Probably a good idea," Drew replied, squeezing himself out from under the woman, embarrassed for his lapse in judgment.

Shark saw the look on his face. "Look man, we got excited for the first time after having a rough time of it," he said, trying to calm Drew's nerves, "let's pack this stuff this up and go home."

By the time Daryl, Drew, and Shark returned to the *Twist,* Drew had already put the incident in the kitchen out of his mind. Today had been another huge win after so many losses. Daryl had radioed back to Crystal and had given her their status and Crystal was already making preparations for their arrival.

She radioed, "Best seafood chef on this island is gonna hook you boys up tonight. And Daryl, you're gonna be getting the best of me afterwards, Uhh-huhh."

Daryl gave Shark a high five and winked at Jeff and Drew as Tom throttled the boat forward back into the Amelia River. His iPhone was now broadcasting "High Heeled Sneakers" and he had it blaring out across the water.

It was good to be on the side of the living.

Chapter 15

As they rounded the north end of Amelia Island and approached Fort Clinch, Tom slowed the boat as the group caught sight of a massive catamaran beached in the sand at the base of the fort.

"Looks like we have a new guest," Tom said.

As the *Twist* pulled into the shallow water, Drew remained tight lipped as he studied the lines of the massive 45 foot catamaran. Her stern announced her as *Delilah*. The other day Drew had not been able to make out the name but he certainly recognized the font.

We meet again, Drew thought to himself.

"The eagle has landed, over," Tom radioed the fort, "Sorry, I have always wanted to say that."

Within minutes it was all hands on deck moving their new haul up and over the outer wall of the fort. The atmosphere was more than pleasant as they had received a hero's welcome when the supplies were unveiled.

Drew's mind was still heavy though and he approached Major Nate who ineffectively was trying to direct the operations that were taking place.

"Major, quite the haul wouldn't you say?" Drew began.

"It's a good day, certainly," he replied putting a hand on Drew's shoulder.

"So, who is our new guest?" Drew asked, pointing over at the hulking *Delilah*.

"Ah, his name is Guy Faulkner, Canadian, an older gent. He arrived just after you guys left this morning. He's in pretty rough shape and didn't have much to say. Seemed a bit shaken up and in need of a good meal so Rose is tending him and we are giving him a spot to himself in the officer's quarters until he regains his strength."

"So what are your thoughts?" Drew asked, seeking more.

"I don't want to formulate any opinions yet because I have not had a chance to really speak with him. Now, help me with this cooler," the Major replied.

The night was clear and brilliant with stars. Josh was playing with Bella in the parade ground as Drew, Tom, Max, Jason, and Major Nate remained around the embers of a bonfire, bellies full of the day's hall and heads swimming with booze. Drew who still refrained, had come to appreciate his sobriety especially given the turn of events over the last week.

The rest of the survivors were either on watch or had called it a night. Crystal had pulled Daryl away earlier and Shark was out walking the inner perimeter with Elizabeth.

"I'm sure we can drum up some more of those AGM batteries but for now this is going to be a good start. You can get six years out of an AGM if properly maintained." Tom said. "We should have everything in place by tomorrow evening if everyone is on board," he continued, looking for a response from the group.

"I can get those wind vanes mounted along with the solar panels first thing in the morning if you can make the connections, Max," Jason said, staring into his drink. "We can also connect the diesel generator to the incoming mains of the fort and probably get lights on in here by tomorrow night," he continued.

"I already was looking at the mains earlier and I think it would be proper to put the batt…" Max started but was caught mid sentence by the fort's newest survivor addition.

Wrapped in a grey blanket that covered his head, a figure appeared in the firelight. Drew saw that he was older, but it was difficult to tell, maybe mid 50s; Shadows deepened the lines in his gaunt face and enhanced the dark circles under his eyes. His beard stubble was as white as the tuft of hair that peeked from under the blanket over his head. Drew thought he looked like one of the Walkers and probably could mosey right out the front gate and mingle with the crowd.

Without introduction, the man said, "Just catching the tail end of this conversation but seems to me we need to put most of our efforts on communications once we can get even the first bit of power on in here."

"Ah, Mr. Faulkner, nice of you to join us. Please have a seat. I take it that your presence here means that you are feeling better and hopefully a bit more rested," Major Nate said, changing subject.

Faulkner remained standing.

Drew stood and held out his hand, introducing himself.

Faulkner returned a weak handshake but did not look at Drew, just kept his gaze on the fire.

"Feeling better, yes, thank you. He coughed a weak

cough and steered the conversation back. "I would like to appoint myself to the communications endeavor. Everyone seems to have their place here, and as we discussed earlier, we all have our jobs to do, to participate that is. I have a network of electronic gear aboard my boat we can use in conjunction with what you already have or can drum up. Seems to me that communications can be our way out of this, surely there are more survivors, probably holed up all over this island. Reaching them could increase our numbers, and possibly our safety. We need to set up the batteries in one of the Commanding officers quarters to keep them away from the elements. In the adjacent room we can set up the communications...."

Drew glanced at Max and could tell he wasn't pleased with a newbie jumping in like this. It may have been the light flickering but it almost looked like Max was also shaking his head in disagreement but he was remaining silent.

What Faulkner was proposing did make sense, the commanding officer's quarters were near the front of the fort on the other side of the sally port from the Guardroom and it was only a short cable run to the incoming main breakers.

Also, the COs quarters was currently unused as it had been staged for tourists. Shark had explained on their tour just the other day, that it had remained vacant due to the noise of the infected amplified by the brick front entrance tunnel. This location also offered more protection from the elements than there would be if they were to set up operations within one of the other buildings. Drew figured Max disagreed because the location wasn't in one of the rear bastions facing the ocean where there would be less effort running the antenna, solar panels, and wind vanes. Even so, placing them on the inland side would protect these from more extreme weather.

Drew could see that this guy was sharp, experienced, and calculating. He was playing chess and had just checkmated Max.

"...And the whir of those vanes along that front wall should silence the noises of those things outside," he continued, pointing along the starlit curtain wall. "Well, I am off to bed, just wanted to say my piece."

Mr. Faulkner glanced in Drew's direction, nodded his nice to meet you, turned, and made his way across the parade ground to the barracks building. Covered still by his blanket, he was a ghost.

"Well, thank you for gracing us with your presence Obie Wan," Jason said, breaking the silence.

Everyone laughed. A couple of drinks seemed to have gotten Jason Freeman out of his shell.

Chapter 16

It was Carey Douglas who discovered her body the next morning. On his hung-over guard patrol along the inner perimeter pathway he found Eileen Simmons hanging by the neck inside the southwest bastion. There was a sign around her neck that read, "my way" and below it, "good luck."

The news quickly spread and deeply affected everyone, but Colonel Wilcox had been the most discouraged by it.

It was not even 10:00 in the morning before they had her buried within the walls of the fort, cleaned up and in a fresh park ranger's uniform.

Colonel Wilcox spoke strong words about the woman and who she was. He spoke of her intensity and her attitude. His respect for her was clearly immense and his tears flowed unchecked down his cheeks as he concluded.

Drew thought about what he had been saying and about the roller coaster they were all on and though not having spent much time with her, he still related to Eileen's desire to get off, to bring this ride to an end. This woman had liked order and control. This new world offered very little promise of either and so she had opted out. She had grabbed control one last time. The night before had been one of celebration and good spirits and she had ended things on a high note, simple as that. Everyone knew it.

And everyone responded. That afternoon individual efforts seemed to have tripled. Those that needed direction took direction without complaint and everyone was pitching in.

Within two hours, Max and Jason had the array of solar panels glinting in the sun from atop the front curtain wall. Within two more, four wind vanes flanked the solar array, two on either side.

As Mr. Faulkner had pointed out, the effect was immediate with the wind vanes dampening the noises from all the commotion on the other side of the wall. It was a blessing. Drew wondered if it would have the reverse effect and the outside numbers would dwindle. This proved to not be the case.

"Nope, no difference, still a shitload of those assholes," he said to himself when he looked out over the wall.

The rotors continued to whir away generating their 24 volts that Drew and Tom had wired down to a voltage regulator in the guard quarters. Tom nodded at Drew with look of satisfaction when the small display read 14.3 volts as the massive dual banks of AGMs were finally boosting.

"Now all we have to worry about is an inverter and we can take care of that tomorrow," Tom said. "For now, let's wire the 12 volt DC into the next room where Guy is putting the comm equipment. By the way, you seen him at all this afternoon Drew?"

"He is down at his boat tearing into things, last I heard. Looks like that means that he's decided to stay," Drew replied.

"Looks like it," Tom returned, unspooling a length of white power cable onto the floor. He immediately stopped when he heard the sputtering of the Kabuta generator as it fired up for the first time.

Tom and Drew rushed outside and around the side of the building to where Shark, Daryl, Jason and Major Nate stood proudly around the running power source.

Everyone was spilling out from their various duties around camp.

"We have light! The kitchen lights are on!" Crystal screamed as she rushed out of her kitchen with Martha Appleman and her husband in tow.

"There is light in the tunnels," Buddy reported, returning from patrol.

Drew radioed Rose up in the infirmary. "Hows things your way Rose? You getting power?"

"Yeah Drew, and a pre-recorded tour or something is now playing in the background– scared the shit out of me when it came on and its kinda creeping me out now."

"Don't worry we will take care of that," Drew radioed back. "Maybe we can hunt down a big screen TV and a Playstation next time we go to town, how does that sound?" Drew said in his elation.

"That works for me, over," Rose returned cheerfully. "I'm sure Josh won't mind either."

"Well we are going to have to regulate our power and fuel usage but we are certainly off to a good start. Speaking of which I think we have done enough work for today," Shark said.

"I heard you on that," Jason said, uncapping his sharpie pen. He wrote "Eileen" on the side of the generator.

By sunset, the party was already in full swing and the bonfire was roaring again alongside the parade ground. Despite events that morning, the mood was cheerful as drinks and food flowed steadily from the kitchen out to the spotlight lit courtyard.

The recorded tour Rose had complained about turned out to be a small ancient boom box that had a battered Maxell cassette on a loop. The small stereo found itself repurposed and was playing an old INXS Kick album, and of course, Shark was dancing around like a maniac.

"Fort Clinch block parties every night baby," he hooted, arms above his head with a drink in one hand and a spliff in the other.

Quite the guy, Drew thought, as he looked through the crowd to Faulkner, who was crossing the parade deck in the direction of the CO quarters where his com room was to be.

"Yo, Mr. Faulkner, come shake what you got baby," Shark called out to him.

Guy Faulkner adjusted the electronic components he held under one arm and raised the other in an acknowledging wave but continued on with his duties.

Shark shrugged off being brushed off and lured Elizabeth into dancing with him.

Tom noticed the exchange and crossed the corner of the parade ground after Faulkner.

Drew followed.

Two quick knocks and the two men entered the comm

room. Guy was already sitting at a wooden desk arranging the cable bundle that dangled from *Delilah*'s recently extracted AIS.

"Hey there Guy, don't you want to give it a rest for a bit today?" Tom started.

"As you can see I have a lot of work to do here," Faulkner replied, continuing with the AIS.

Tom stepped forward and put his hand on Faulkner's shoulder, "Look, today was a huge success and I'm just saying maybe you should pace yourself a bit or…"

Faulkner cut him off and rose to his feet.

"A success? What I see is a bunch of people that don't seem to have a clue as to the seriousness of this situation. Getting communications up is critical and I already see that the 12 volt supply still has not been completed…"

"Hold up right there…" Tom started.

Drew could see redness deepening in his already tanned face.

Tom resigned and put up his hands in the air in dismissal.

"I'm not even gonna respond," he said and headed back toward the door. He turned before leaving, "maybe you should show some gratitude toward the people that took you in," and with that, Tom was gone.

Faulkner looked over at Drew and then to the floor. There was silence for a moment.

"So why did you shoot at me?" Drew asked.

Faulkner looked up in surprise as if being slapped, "What are you talking about?"

"The other day, I even tried to radio you but got no response," Drew went on.

Faulkner had a searching look on his face but Drew could see that he was putting it together now.

"You remembering now? Monohull sailboat? I tried to radio you?"

"ok, yes, I…" Faulkner said, looking sheepish.

He didn't look at Drew but turned and continued with the AIS. "…well you don't know who you can trust right now. The world is a much different place."

Drew felt anger raging up inside him but maintained his cool.

"Keep in mind your coming here says to me that you did trust us, but your attitude tells a different tale," Drew said and began to head out the door. "I won't say anything about it to the others and I will see that someone brings you a plate of food."

Drew stepped outside onto the parade ground not wanting to hear any response from Faulkner.

Back outside the party was still in full swing and despite what Faulkner said, there was reason to celebrate. The grounds were lit and it was a beautiful sight at night. There was a new festiveness to the place that soaked into you. It felt truly safe for the first time.

Instead of returning to the festivities, Drew crossed the parade ground away from the action and decided to relieve Buddy from his position guarding the wall. He felt he wanted some alone time and figured Buddy deserved some of his own time to take part in the ruckus that Shark still led.

It appeared Bella had given up on the party as well. She spotted Drew and raced across the parade ground after him in a tri-color flash.

"Walking the wall," as it had come to being called,

consisted of making a loop around the fort via the path between the outer rampart and curtain wall, checking the walls and bastion window-slits for damage. Once the loop was made, you made your way up to the terreplein and patrolled above, looking for potentially threatening congregations of the infected. It was highly unlikely that even one of the Drinkers would be able to come over the top of the wall, but patrolling it still brought peace of mind to the camp. It also wasn't a job for the timid or squeamish, Drew thought, as he entered the south bastion.

Inside, the lights pulsed in sync with the generator as the creatures spotted Drew and Bella's presence immediately through the balistraria in the bastion wall. Soon, all four arrow slits were filled with decomposing flesh trying to work its way in.

Bella had her hackle up and was growling steadily. Drew noticed she had lost some of the tendency to bark whenever she came upon the monsters.

One in particular was attempting to push its face between the weather beaten brick. Drew could hear the bones in its face cracking as it tried to come through the tight opening.

He illuminated its face with a small led penlight and checked the surrounding brick for damage. It would hold for now, but eventually weeks of the constant scraping and tearing at the old brick and mortar would begin to cause things to fail. Keeping an eye on it was the right plan. Drew switched off the penlight and stepped back out into the night air. Bella stood her ground for a second but then scurried after him.

"Maybe we should change 'walking the wall' back to a two man job," he said to Bella as he followed the path behind the old latrines toward the southwest bastion. "or at least one man and a dog," he said giving her an appreciative pat on her head. It was funny that a 6 pound dog could pack so much comfort.

Suddenly her ears perked up and she suddenly started barking.

Drew heard the dogs too. It sounded like several of them on the other side of the wall.

Quickly, Drew grabbed up Bella and climbed the earthen embankment up onto the top of the terreplein to get a better view. Bella was squirming, anxious to get free.

There were three of them, two black labs and a shepherd mix. They had apparently taken advantage of the distraction caused by Drew's presence in the bastion and had brought a Walker to the ground and were tearing at it while dodging advances of the Drinkers. They barked and lunged at them but interestingly kept their distance as if sensing the disease. They had no problem working at the Walker that was fighting to stand. In the dim glow of starlight Drew watched as they brought him down and jerked strips of rotten flesh from his leg muscles. Even in this visibility, Drew could see that one of the dogs, the shepherd mix, still had a collar on, its metal tags flashing in the starlight. Someone's pet.

"Must have run out of Purina," Rose said, startling Drew from behind. "I saw you two up here looking at something and came to check it out."

"God Rose, you scared me." Drew said, heart recovering. "You don't want to see this."

"You're the one that scared," Rose said and poked his side.

"Well–uh...," Drew pretended to clear his throat and mumbled playfully to himself.

The three of them stood looking out at the excitement on the other side of the wall. Bella had quit barking and watched, head cocked, with composed curiosity.

"You know, it actually doesn't bother me." Rose said.

"What's that?" Drew responded.

"Seeing that," Rose nodded in the direction of the dog that finally had the corpse's arms free. It skittered off and made its way into the shadows of the woods with the appendage dangling from its mouth. The hand waved its last goodbye is it disappeared into the darkness.

"Seems like we are always afraid of things at first, but then you just get used to them. It becomes part of the norm, you know?" Rose explained.

"I can tell you I am still in the getting used to it stage, myself," Drew responded, "You say that you're getting used to it but you have to make sure your being used to it doesn't mean you are becoming complacent." Drew added.

"Complacent?" Rose asked.

"Just don't let your guard down," Drew said.

"'Situational awareness,' Major Nate calls it." Rose returned, "I already had this discussion with him."

"I meant you no disrespect," Drew apologized. "I clearly see you are cut from a different cloth."

Rose raised her rifle and put a round through the head of a Drinker chasing one of the labs.

Bella flinched and let out a small yip at the sound of the weapon.

Drew took his hands from his ears, "What are you gonna do when you run out of ammo?" He said as Rose racked back the bolt, ejecting the brass onto the ground.

"Get a bigger gun," she replied.

Chapter 17

It was mid-morning the next day when the *Twist* was back out on the water, headed east out of the Cumberland Sound, around past the jetties, and into the Atlantic Ocean. There wasn't a cloud in the sky and the sea was a lake, good conditions to survey the Atlantic side of the island.

Bella made the cut with Drew the previous night and was now on the team. She made up for the skeleton crew that consisted of Tom at the helm, Shark and Drew. Daryl and Jeff remained behind because Crystal and Elizabeth refused to let them come along. The ladies were worried because if anything were to happen to the boat, you would be exposed and washing ashore would be a death sentence due to the miles of sandy beaches and housing along the waterfront. It would be easier contending with one of the Drinkers, than contending with Elizabeth or Crystal if something were to happen to the men in their lives. That being said, the men had remained behind to help with the fort's new "grid." It made sense but also made Drew feel alone in a way. Well, at least he did have Bella, he thought, looking over at her on the cockpit bench. The breeze blew her hair back on her face making her look like a ferret. He could tell she was happy to be out on the water again.

"I noticed that Elizabeth really wasn't too keen on you coming either there big man," Drew nudged Shark as the *Twist* hugged the shoreline. All eyes seemed to move between the depth finder and the beach where the Drinkers made their way to the sand in response to the noise coming off the twin Mercs.

"She is way out of Marky Mark's league," Tom spoke up.

Drew laughed and Shark playfully shoved him.

"You guys can go fuck yourselves," he said, allowing his expression to give away the crush he had on Jeff's mom.

"Well gent's, we are approaching Main Beach," Tom said bringing their fishing boat to what Drew felt was dangerously close to shore.

Bella darted up to the bow with her teeth bared.

"This is the main public beach access. That's a park and a miniature golf place–and to the left there," he pointed, "is a restaurant. If you look straight ahead that road cuts clear across to downtown. A little bit up and to the right is the entrance road to the fort, a three mile stretch, in case you ever need it," Tom added.

From what Drew could tell there must have been a decent amount of activity at this main public access when things had changed. Cars were parked in the lot in front of "Sandy Bottoms," a waterfront restaurant that was now permanently closed. A number of Walkers tried to negotiate around the rusty chain link fence that surrounded a weathered Putt-Putt golf course. Desperate looking Drinkers sprinted their way down to shore, stopping again, only knee deep in the sea, frustrated by the floating meal just yards away.

"What we are dealing with here?" Tom said, "Let's just

see how well this fishing boat trolls for Zombies."

With that he leaned forward and switched on the boat's ridiculous stereo. Shrill harmonica immediately pierced the air as Ozzy Ozbourne launched into "The Wizard."

Randy Rhodes was not half way through his guitar solo before at least a hundred of the infected had gathered for the concert.

Tom muted the music.

"Looks like a no go for Main Beach and it will probably be like this the entire way down the east coast," he commented and turned the *Twist* south.

They continued down the coastline. The tide was approaching high and had a tendency to conceal sandbars so they kept their speed down. If you were to get hung up at high tide that meant you were completely fucked. It was interesting to see the endurance of the Drinkers along the beach. As their boat cruised along, the Drinkers would rush the beach from the various coastal vacation homes, emerging from the dunes, and from along the tops of weathered wooden walkways. They cascaded down onto the sand in pursuit of the passing vessel. Some would make it out into the surf to their knees but the seemingly more intelligent ones were staying on the beach unimpeded by the surf and able to track along with their boat. They seemed to retain about the same endurance of the average person–It only made sense though, why should they have more? It wasn't like they had received superhuman powers. After about a quarter mile they would buckle over gasping for air, eyes never leaving the prize. Regaining stamina, they would make another attempt until their dinner plans were long out of reach.

"They sure are determined," Drew said pointing at one that seemed to be even more agitated than the rest. It was a heavier set Drinker in a business suit, totally overdressed for the occasion. "He must have turned more recently because he is a real tweaker."

"Maybe so, I have noticed that our old girl Heidi, back at the fort has kinda lost the twinkle in her eye. I think not eating may actually take the fight out of them after time. I'm not saying we should be inviting her out for a drink, I'm just saying she isn't chomping at the little window as much," Shark commented.

"It only makes sense after seeing them run that starving the Drinkers would cause them to fatigue just the same. The Walkers are already in low gear. I don't know for sure, but I imagine that they have to run out of food sometime. Eventually, I would think they may pose no more threat than a regular Walker and that could be only in a matter of a couple more weeks," Drew said.

"Well that would be nice, 'cause any food to be found in those houses ain't getting any fresher," Tom added.

"What about thirst? Drew asked. "How is our girl getting along without water?"

"You don't know?" Shark said, "She's been pissing herself and drinking it off of the floor," he said, raising Drew's green binoculars and scanning the shoreline. "She is a real prize, that one. I can tell you I ain't taking her out for a bathroom break though."

"Oh Jesus, seriously? I guess that does take some of the charm away from her now." Drew replied.

"Ahead is the Sadler road beach access. That building to the right is a Sliders Oyster Bar. Our salesman of the year there was probably having a power lunch when this all went down. Across the roundabout from it is a biker bar and a small beach store, "Halls," I think it's called. That road that leads out from the roundabout bisects the island and eventually leads to the bridge at the Yacht Basin where we scored the batteries. There are a couple of hotels in this area and this is a fairly busy intersection. I wanna give it another go with the stereo and see what's what," Tom said.

The speakers boomed to life again.

This time it was Drivin' N' Cryin' drawing them out with "Straight to Hell."

"Yo this is my jam, an oldie but a goodie," Shark said, leaning forward and turning up the volume as the masses ambled down the beach access toward them.

Drew felt grateful for not having to do anything like this alone. He looked over at Shark who seemed more focused on the stereo than the horror out in front of them. It was contagious. They were all at ease for no other reason than each other. Even with little Bella, this would be unbearable single-handed. If you were the last survivor on the globe what would be the point of survival? The peace he felt came from the fact that if he were to die he probably wouldn't be doing so alone. That had been the appeal of the fort. There was an allegiance now and these were his brothers, the fort had quickly become his new family and his home.

"This is like feeding seagulls," Tom said turning down the music. "We show up with a couple of those things hanging around and word travels fast amongst those freaks. You can feed a single gull with none others in site and before you know it, within seconds, there is a swarm."

"Yeah, only these gulls will do more damage than just shit on your head," Shark added.

"Even with your seagull effect, I'm still not seeing as many as I would have expected," Drew said, pointing at a crowd of about 50 or so, congregating at the beach. "There are not nearly as many as there are downtown."

"Well, island population is just under 12,000, last I checked. From the cars that were parked coming and going on the Shave bridge, I assume people didn't know where to go so population numbers probably have never changed all that much from when this thing broke out. Many people are probably trapped inside their homes as infected, or have possibly survived. There is no telling. What I imagine is that there is a large group or groups of them swarming at various locations, chasing some common goal, like us with the radio. They may even be in numbers that resemble what it looks like downtown," Tom suggested. "Let's roll" he said, throttling the sport-fisher on further south.

As they continued, they occasionally passed a Walker but the beaches seemed to be clear for the most part. It was eerie.

They approached a fishing pier that jutted out to sea from the first of two dark condominium buildings that loomed in the distance. A hunter 380 sailboat, *Second Wind,* was dismasted and lodged between the pilings toward the end of the pier where it terminated into a T.

"What do you guys think? Tom said approaching the wreck.

"Looks like there was trouble and she eventually drifted down and got caught up..."

"Never mind that, check it out, the pier," Drew pointed. "I'm not seeing any of the freaks. Pull alongside the Hunter. There is no movement aboard from what I can tell."

Bella didn't seem to be alarmed and they all eyeballed her as much as they did the depth meter.

Tom blew the *Twist of Fate*'s air horn as the three kept an eye on the pier and the sailboat.

Still nothing.

"Take it easy bro," Drew called after Shark who leapt the gap over to the stranded sailboat. Shark's added weight shifted the boat and caused its bilge pumps to come on. It would be only a matter of time before she was on the bottom.

Gun drawn, Shark scrambled into the cockpit and was looking into the companionway.

"It's clear," Shark said aloud and disappeared into the cabin.

On the side of the pier Drew noticed a wooden ladder that ran up to the deck above. He crossed over the bow of the Hunter and started up. The lower rungs were so encrusted with barnacles that his foot slipped and they scraped through his uniform wool trousers into his shin like razors.

"Dammit," he said feeling blood flow into his sock.

From behind him, Bella was barking in disapproval.

"You sure you wanna be up there Drew? You seem to be the one that needs to take it easy," Tom called from below.

"It's all good. If I see any trouble I will hop over the rail. Just come get me, please." Drew called down.

"Oh, hell yes," Shark called from the sailboat's cabin. He surfaced with a Ziplock and held it out through the companionway. We got weed, fellas."

"Looks like shitty old shake to me," Tom said.

"It is my friend, and I wouldn't trade it for an ounce of finest Crippy around my man," Shark said, cheerfully emerging into the cockpit.

"Shit weed means seeds, and seeds mean crops and I can't wait until spring," he said, more thoroughly inspecting the baggie in the sunlight.

"Alright, alright, Cheech, what else you find? Tom asked.

"Couple cans of food, six pack of beer, and a couple bottles of booze." Shark called up from the cabin as he rifled through things below. "There is also a 12 volt NAXA TV/DVD player combo and a binder of movies, kids back at the fort may get a kick out of that."

Drew wasn't interested in the conversation below as he hopped over the railing and dropped into a crouch with his weapon drawn. Despite not seeing anyone up the length of pier, his heart was pounding in his chest. Staying low made him feel safer and would help him spring over the railing and into the ocean in a matter of seconds.

About midway down the pier where it passed over land, Drew's anxiety was reaching an apex. At the end of the pier he could see that there was a metal 8 foot gate that was closed and securely locked. He wondered how many infected the bars would hold back because from the looks of them, they were more than likely made of aluminum.

He scanned the condominium complex. From this distance he was able to see that several sliding glass doors and windows had been broken in both buildings but the balconies remained vacant, all but for a lone elderly female Walker on a high floor that just gazed out at nothingness. She hadn't taken notice of Drew.

As he approached the gate, he was able to see into the pool area. Several bodies lay motionless below on the concrete patio, their heads opened up in a brownish mess mostly picked apart by gulls. They looked to have gone over the metal balcony rails. Probably infected and disoriented they had met their conclusion poolside.

Immediately, he spotted a pair of Walkers making it

around the side of the building. They had taken notice of him and ambled toward the gate.

That was enough to make Drew head back to the boat at a quick jog. As he returned to the *Twist*, Drew turned and watched them at the gate. It was locked and holding well but he wasn't taking any chances. When he made it back to the end of the pier, he descended the ladder and boarded the *Twist* just as Shark was bringing aboard the meager supplies from the Hunter.

"At least we also got another two batteries. That means this old Hunter will be home to the fishies before sundown," Shark said, untying from the foundering vessel whose bilge pumps were now silent again.

"Let's continue on. If we are still gonna go all the way around the island, we have some ground to cover before sundown," Tom said.

Further down the beach, there was a shrimp boat stranded onshore, its booms were still swung out and nets lay in a tangled mess alongside its rust streaked hull. Half buried in the sand, they anchored the boat in place.

"From about where that shrimp boat is to the southern tip of the island your looking at the resort areas, five star hotels, condos and such." Tom pointed out.

"Sorry I didn't bring my fancy shoes." Shark said holding his nose in the air in feigned sophistication and lighting his one-hitter.

"Well, it will probably be quite a bit more festive there." Drew added.

"Probably so, that area stays busy pretty much year

round," Tom agreed, but as they skirted the coastline it wasn't quite the case. There was an occasional Walker migrating blindly down the beach toward them but they hadn't seen a Drinker since the *Glengarry Glen Ross* freak in the suit, back at Sliders.

"Dude what is the deal here?" Shark said, turning up the radio as they passed what Tom pointed out to be the Amelia Island Plantation. "Here Zombie, Zombie," he called out over Jimmy Buffet's "Cheeseburger in Paradise."

Even still, only a handful of Walkers had responded and materialized on the beach near their location.

"This just ain't right," Drew commented.

"Let's give it a minute," Tom said, slowing the boat to an idle.

Suddenly, waves of Drinkers finally poured out onto the sand in response to the blaring JL audios. Within minutes the shoreline was filling in. There were already at least 300 Drinkers onshore and a mass of at least a thousand Stage-2s picking up the rear-streaming from between buildings and down wooden boardwalks.

"It's the Buffet that's doing it. Draws rich old yankee snowbirds every time. Fuck gents, look at all of them," Shark said.

"It is more of the buffet aboard this boat than the Buffett," Drew said to himself, mesmerized by the sea of monsters in front of them. It was a mishmash of infected in various states of disrepair representing all levels of social status. They now all worked toward the same common goal.

"Well, I think this party is about over," Tom said, turning off the radio and heading their boat out to deeper water and toward the southern tip of this island.

As they sped away the infected seemed to have lost focus

on their prize which was now clearly out of reach.

Further south, the island offered a long stretch of empty beach that jutted out and didn't show much sign of life, or death. A white 4x4 Toyota Tacoma with a magnetic beach patrol sign sat quietly near the dense tree line and a bright red Honda quad lay on its side nearby.

Drew was the first to spot a number of rectangular, maroon objects strewn along the shoreline.

"What do you suppose those are?" Drew said.

"No telling," Shark responded.

Just as they rounded the tip Tom slowed the boat to a crawl. "Holy fucking shit, will you look at that," Shark came again.

The four of them stared in silence at the two parallel bridges that joined Amelia Island with Big Talbot Island, its southerly neighbor in the chain. The destruction was magnificent.

"That flight was probably a departure from Jacksonville International Airport." Tom said, as they approached the wreckage. The plane they were looking at had been heading east, made contact with newer main bridge and had wiped out a large center mass section with its field of debris. A massive piece of tail section was hanging precariously off the Amelia side of the gap in the road that it had created. Even with the charred result of the fuel tanks exploding, Drew could still see through to the Delta blue logo on what was left of its rudder. The tubular fuselage had broken apart on impact and sunk into the channel. The concrete from the roadway above had come down on top of it, pinning it in a saltwater grave.

As they moved forward, entering the gap in the span, they could see into the dangling tail section above them. Several rows of charred, bird scavenged bodies remained suspended upside down still strapped in their maroon leather chairs.

"Seat cushions," that's what we were seeing earlier along the beach," Drew said.

Seagulls stood glaring at them from above, perched high on the jagged roadway as Tom negotiated the *Twist* through the span. "Well, we know one thing now." Drew spoke up again.

"What's that?" Shark asked.

"Take a look at the old fishing bridge running parallel to the main one here. Looks like it was being worked on, that metal center span is swung open on its pivot point. We should be safe to assume that there is a determinate number of infected on the island if your telling me that this is the only other access. That bridge at the yacht basin was a no go with all the vehicles jammed up across the span," Drew explained.

Bella wined loudly as she looking up at the infected that were now congesting along the guardrails above as they passed between the two bridge spans.

"So, not trying to jump ahead and read your mind, but are you about to propose we start sweeping the island until they are all wiped out?" Shark asked.

"I think that would be out of the question. We have an area the geographical size of Manhattan with plenty of places for those things to be hiding out," Drew responded.

The marine radio popped and went to fuzz. All eyes locked onto the green LCD screen that registered channel 16.

"Shit, is someone trying to broadcast?", Tom said turning up the volume and adjusting squelch. "We are way out of range of the fort."

It came again, a pop, and then fuzz, and then silence.

Once more the pop came, and fuzz, then "...Carl..."

"Carl?" Drew said.

"what the fuck?" Shark said, leaning forward to await another transmission.

None came.

"Fellas, I think I got it, and we are just out of range," Tom said, immediately throttling the boat from between the span and back around the southern tip of the island from where they came.

Bella lost her footing at the sudden change in motion and dashed to the security of Drew's lap.

"So you gonna fill us in Tom?" Shark asked, looking over at Drew with a puzzled expression on his face.

"Just bear with me," Tom said, as the boat picked up speed. He grabbed the VHF handheld and spoke. "This is the fishing vessel *Twist of Fate* please repeat your transmission."

Silence

Tom said again, "This is the fishing vessel *Twist of Fate*, please repeat your transmission.

Drew looked back at Shark, returning an equal expression of confusion.

Tom appeared to have a destination in mind as they headed northward. Within minutes they saw a greasy plume of smoke rising high in the air that seemed to confirm Tom's hunch as they slowed the boat in front of a large U shaped resort they had previously motored past.

"Ritz Carlton, this is the fishing vessel *Twist of Fate* please repeat your transmission, over," Tom said.

Drew squinted toward the roof of the luxurious building as rancid looking smoke rose into the sky from a small fire on top. He couldn't tell from this distance but it appeared to be a controlled burn.

He saw movement on the rooftop under a covered area at the base of the U. Then, there was activity along the top floor balconies. Survivors.

Suddenly, the infected began to appear on many of the oceanfront balconies across the entire backside of the hotel and he noticed the nightmare horde of infected in the grounds below that had been partially blocked by the beachfront dunes. Upon their arrival, the horde had taken notice of the approaching boat and many were already making their way through toppled poolside cabanas, beach chairs and sunbrellas, down to the shoreline.

The radio came in clear.

"*Twist of Fate*, we read you loud and clear," a man's voice responded.

Drew counted three figures running along the rooftop toward the northern side of the building.

"This is John Summerland head of security here, can you report you status and intention, over?"

"This is Tom White…uh, our status and intention?" Tom radioed back. "Well, our intention is to respond to your signal, so I'm gonna ask you back, what's your status and intention? John, Over."

Tom looked at Drew and Shark and shrugged. He was smiling.

The three men had reached the edge of the rooftop but from this distance, looking into the setting sun, Drew was unable to make out any of their features.

Several top floor balconies had filled at this point, uninfected figures leaning out over the rails to get a better view of their boat while the infected on the balconies below reached up at them.

"Tom, we are 23 strong: 9 women, 10 men, and 4 children. We have been here since this thing started and have taken many losses. Our supplies are dwindling and our situation is not sustainable for any extended period, maybe three weeks. We have been able to secure the top floor of the building but as you can clearly see the rest of the hotel is overrun," John said.

"Sounds like you have your hands full. I thought it wasn't possible, but I have to say we are a little better off. I am part of a group of survivors that came together at Fort Clinch. We have 14 survivors, 6 men, 6 women, a teenage girl, and a young boy." Tom looked at Bella, "and a Chihuahua," he added. "I think that I can speak for the group and extend your party an invitation but I'm not quite sure what to say about your current dilemma."

Tom looked at Drew and Shark who responded with nods of agreement. "We have adequate security, space, food, water and supplies, but I got to say your situation is pretty intense, over," Tom continued as he looked out at the gathering nightmare on the beach.

"Yes, it sure is, over," John replied.

There was silence on both ends of the radio.

Drew spoke up. "You know we are gonna have to help them."

"Well, I'm not sure how we would pull it off without it turning into a suicide mission for everyone involved, Shark said. "I got tricks up my sleeve but I'm no magician."

Tom spoke into the radio, "John, it's getting late and we need to return to Fort Clinch. We will be back."

"I appreciate your optimism," John replied. "Godspeed, over."

With that, Tom put the boat in gear and started north.

The radio came on and John came across again,"I just have to ask, is there a man named Jim Sloan in your group?" John asked.

"Alive and well," Tom said.

"That is good to hear, thank you Tom. Goodnight, over," John said.

"Goodnight to you as well," Tom closed, returning the handheld to the mount as they motored toward the darkening skyline.

It was pitch black by the time the *Twist* was back at the fort. Tom had radioed ahead of time and spoke with Sergeant Sloan of their incoming arrival and had briefed him ahead of time on the discovery of survivors. As Tom guided the boat in, a small party was standing on the beach to greet them, Sergeant Sloan, Major Nate, Daryl, Jeff and Elizabeth.

Lights were on in *Delilah* and Faulkner emerged from the cabin of his massive sailboat as the *Twist* pulled beside him.

Clearly, everyone was very anxious to hear about the survivors in the Ritz Carlton and Drew understood why. It offered promise. "The more the merrier," it seemed.

"Evening folks," Shark spoke first, stepping onto the sandy beach.

"Sounds like my pal John gave you guys quite a surprise," Sergeant Sloan said.

"He sure did," Tom said, "and your friend has found himself in quite a predicament."

"Sergeant Bill, you know the guy over at the Ritz?" Jeff

spoke up, helping Shark secure the *Twist*.

"We go to the same church together, St Peter's Episcopal down on Main Street. A good man. He's been the head of security at the Ritz since the doors opened in the late 90's," Bill explained. "Tom, you said there are 23 people over there? On the top floor?"

"That is about the gist of it from our short conversation. He said the top floor was secure and they had survivors and sustainability of about 3 weeks. I hate to disappoint everyone but we really don't know much more," Tom answered. "Their building is under siege and there are hundreds of infected there. We should be thankful for our situation here."

"Will there be any attempt at rescue?" Faulkner interrupted, leaning against the hard dodger of his catamaran.

"We can't say what the plan will be and I'm not sure we would know where to begin but I think we need to do something," Drew answered.

Faulkner responded with a nod and disappeared back inside his yacht.

"Fucking freak," Drew heard Jeff mutter under his breath.

Jeff's mom glared at him and he responded by rolling his eyes.

Crystal appeared at the top of the northwest bastion.

"Are you all gonna stand out in the cold talking or come in and get some of the dinner I been working on all afternoon?" she asked.

Late that night, rain struck the ancient glass windows of

the enlisted barracks as Drew sat at a small pine desk staring out at the parade ground. He couldn't sleep. Max Dipace was currently at the front entrance on guard duty leaning under the portico smoking a cigarette and lights were on in the "communications room" as it appeared Faulkner was up burning the midnight oil as well.

Drew's concerns however, were the people at the Ritz. During dinner, the whole group had brought possibilities of their rescue, but due to the nature of the situation, everything appeared to be the suicide mission that Shark had spoken of. Sergeant Sloan had said that the top floor was the club level and that there was a kitchen and bar area that had probably provided them food and water. There were also 40 plus rooms with minibars.

"Not sure how they are gonna survive off of candy bars, peanuts, mini bottles, and four dollar bottles of water for the next three weeks, but I trust that Mr. Summerland has everything under control up there," Bill had said.

Even still, those people needed rescue and for Drew, this sense of obligation was the source of his insomnia.

Again, he closed his eyes, mapping out the place from the photograph he had taken in his mind. Too fucking bad the internet was down and he couldn't just check things out on Google earth. Even if you did have some crazy zip-line thing rigged up as Tom had suggested, what would it be like bringing down those small children? Even if you had vehicles, tanks even, and drove right up to the front door, those freaks would blanket you. Loss of visibility alone would cripple you in a mob of rot and stink. Drew wondered what it had been like over there. How had they managed to secure the top floor? He could speculate it all night long but he just figured that when things broke out most of those on the top floor had just remained where they were.

They probably assumed that they could just wait it out. After all why leave? You were in paradise, you had money, and things that were happening amongst the hoi polloi were certainly horrible but unlikely to reach you. That actually had been the case at first, but it turned out to become their prison. If John Summerland was able to maintain the wellbeing of that group under those conditions then he was every bit of the man that Bill Sloan said he was.

Fuck, what to do? Drew pondered.

"What are you still doing up?" Shark asked as he entered the room, irreverently kicking off his sodden brogans.

"Still at it, you know?" Drew responded, sketching out a map of the building as he remembered it.

"Yea, I do," Shark returned.

Drew could tell by Shark's dreamy demeanor that he had been out with Jeff's mom that night but didn't bring it up. Shark wasn't one to kiss and tell, and despite his antics he was a class act-at least in that way. Drew respected him for it. It did make him sick for his own wife seeing Shark's rough edges go smooth over the last couple of days, but he was happy for him. Jeff's mom would certainly have her hands full he thought, smiling to himself.

"You come up with anything yet?" Shark asked.

"No, same ideas resulting in the same problems," he returned.

"Well, look Drew, we will go back tomorrow and take another look. For now, we are useless without sleep," Shark encouraged, as he stripped off his sweat stained tee shirt and climbed into his bunk.

Chapter 18

The nights drizzle only brought thunderstorms the next morning, and it was Tom that pulled the plug on another trip along the Atlantic coast. He was actually reluctant to go anywhere that morning, but they needed to be making constant supply runs and the rest of the group had to convince him of it. Once again, it was the regular crew: Daryl, Drew, Tom and Shark. Bella was back at the fort with Josh and Jeff had wanted to come along, but Shark said no due to the conditions. He was lucky he wasn't with them, Drew thought, as the fishing boat pitched around in the rough currents of the Amelia Sound.

With Tom at the helm again, they headed to a small marina and yacht club isolated on a small island on the mainland side nearly adjacent to downtown Fernandina. A small inlet led them back to A-dock, the first of five concrete docks that made up the Oyster Bay Yacht Club. Only a handful of small pleasure boats occupied the slips here. The whole group seemed relieved that the surrounding marshland offered much relief from the churning intercostal waterway, especially Daryl who still looked green, despite his natural-born complexion. The place looked eerily quiet as they pulled alongside A-dock, ensuring that they had quick exit if need be.

"This place should be pretty quiet fellas, but keep alert," Tom said and let off a short burst from his air horn.

A minute or so passed and there was no noticeable response.

"Kinda what I expected. This is at the far end of a small upper middle class community that is–well, was–still being built out. Being that it's winter, I don't believe anyone would have been at the pool and the clubhouse right now was more of a real estate office than a functional gathering spot. A small bridge leads out to this island so there shouldn't be any surprises, but again, be on your guard."

This time it was Shark who remained in the boat. Tom took the lead as he knew this marina well and he explained how he had helped advise on it's licensing as he, Drew, and Daryl made their way slowly down the pier that led to the clubhouse in the distance.

Giant live oaks loomed overhead and it reminded Drew of the house back on Cat Island. He felt the hairs on his arms begin to stand on end but then breathed a sigh of relief as his nerves were calmed when they reached a locked gate at the end of the pier next to a Tiki-hut bar.

Just beyond, was a circular driveway with only a lone SUV, a black Lexus 470 parked forever and already showing signs of neglect. It leaned at a dramatic angle on its flattened driver side rear tire.

"That's Charlotte Wilkin's Lexus; she ran the real estate office here," Tom said, pressing the gate code buttons.

"It's 2 and 3 at the same time and then 1. Remember it," he instructed.

Swinging the gate open, they raised their weapons as they crossed the parking lot to the brick paved drive of the Marina Clubhouse.

"You guys head on, I will watch the bridge," Daryl said. "Tom, hand me that air horn. Look, one blast will mean we need to leave. Two blasts means we need to get the fuck out."

"Gotcha," Drew said and followed Tom up the circular brick drive to the Clubhouse.

It was a modern and fresh new two story building with dark grey paneled siding and a red barrel tiled roof. The tall upper floor windows had tall white hurricane shutters that were drawn tightly shut. The drive they were on circled under the overhanging upper floor and marked the grand front entrance to the facility. Approaching, Drew noticed greasy stains surrounding the entire bottom portion of the building.

"Looks like they tried to get in," Drew said, pointing out the front door. The varnish on the outside had been clawed down to splinters but the door still held firmly in place.

"Maybe they did," Tom returned, heading around the right side of the building, leading them up a staircase to the upper pool deck area. The full length glass windows that once surrounded the entire backside of the building here were in shards strewn across the wooden patio, they snapped and popped under their feet as they entered a main dining room area.

Drew clenched his teeth with every step and it felt like the handle of the 1911 would turn into a diamond if he clutched it any tighter. Despite the cold air whipping through the open room, sweat dripped into his eyes.

"Where the fuck are they now? There must have been

dozens of them in here at one time," Tom said, pointing the barrel of his gun at the brown, blood soaked carpeting.

"I don't know, but from the looks of it we may have a survivor." Drew said and crossed the room to a bar that opened out in to the main dining room. A metal blind on rollers was pulled down and firmly attached to the polished granite countertop. The infected had been able to cave it inward but the bar height had restricted their ability to put their weight against it and it held secure. The metal kitchen door to the left of it had a circular safety glass window and Drew could see there was something that had been moved behind it, blocking its ability to open. There was no other visible entrance.

Drew tapped his Colt on the rolling shutter above the bar.

"Hello? Is there anyone in there?" He reluctantly called out.

"Watch my back and I will take care of that lock," Tom said, smashing the butt of his rifle against the Master.

"Fuck that's loud," Drew said. He cringed and held his breath.

Two more strikes and it came free.

They both paused and listened. The only sound was the rain striking the water in the pool outside and the rustle of oak leaves in the breeze.

Drew looked at Tom and exhaled with a sigh.

Tom struggled with the warped metal door and was able to create a three foot gap above the bar. The combined smell of rotten food and death that wafted out was a knockout blow. Tom put his hand to his nose and mouth and peered in as Drew shined his penlight inside.

"Looks all clear," Drew said, sliding over the bar into the dark kitchen. "Keep an eye on things out there for me."

Stainless steel glinted in the light from the small LED Mag as Drew eyes adjusted to his surroundings. The place was a disaster. Pots and pans filled the sink and were strewn across the floor. Cabinet doors hung open exposing opened canned goods that reeked of the putrid contents, congealing inside.

There was a small prep island in the middle of the room and Drew paused the light on an unmolested wineglass and an empty bottle of Rosemont Shiraz. Parked next to it was a small Sterno cooking setup on the butcher block surface.

More adrenaline injected into his system as he shined past the prep station to the closed walk in door at the other side of the room. Its porthole window was dark and lifeless.

"Tom, we actually may have a survivor in here." Drew called out quietly. He could feel his finger tightening on the trigger as he carefully approached the walk in, feet making tracks on the Spanish tile floor in spilled flour that seemed to blanket everything.

"Hello?" He called through the door.

There was no response.

Using the toe of his Sperry's, he nudged the door open. Immediately he saw the body of a woman lying motionless on the floor.

"Looks like I may have found your lady. She's dead." Drew gave update, entering the large pantry.

Beside her lay the contents of a purse; car keys, makeup and business cards.

Drew picked up her wallet and verified ID. It was indeed Tom's friend and she had indeed apparently had survived the infection at least for some time, but Drew couldn't see any cause of death. Curious, she had not turned, but suicide? There didn't appear to be any signs of it from what Drew could tell.

Whatever happened she must have had a hell of a time in here, he thought. Alone, in the dark, those things banging on the metal door relentlessly, Jesus. How long had she lasted?

Drew put a light on the woman's face.

From the looks of it, maybe not that long. Tendrils of salt and pepper hair framed her gaunt face. Her skin was leathery and pulled tight against her features. Eyes sunken in and Shiraz stained, chapped lips seemed to tell a tale of thirst and dehydration. Other than that, she didn't seem to have any advanced stages of decomposition and she smelled more like sweat and human discharge than decay.

We were too late, Drew thought. We could have saved her.

He illuminated the room shelved in a massive supply of sundries. There was enough to eat for weeks but wasn't anything at all to drink. She had gone through all of that. Littered across black rubber floor mat were empty water bottles and discarded cans of soda and beer. As he surveyed the room he noticed that every container that had contained fluid was breached down to a large can of peaches that had been punctured with just two small holes for evacuating the fluid. What a horrible way to go. Monsters had been at the door and just beyond them, a swimming pool of possibly sterile, crystal clear water.

This was a tough lady.

"I'm sorry I didn't get to you earlier," he said covering her with an apron he found hanging on the shelf above.

Drew turned his attention back to the task at hand and filled his duffel bag with what he could find and headed back into the kitchen. On his way out, he shined his light on the empty wine glass and then over to the sink. Slow drips were forming at the faucet then dropping into a large saucepan below.

This woman hadn't just been strong; she had been hard as a rock and clearly had been informed as to the source of the infection. It made Drew wish even more that she had been alive when he found her. His group needed people like that. How many more were out there suffering this same fate? Drew hated this, hated the unfairness, and hated the frustration. He was angry. It welled up in him and was replacing the emptiness he had felt for so long, it pulled hard at him, offered release, offered strength, power, and control.

Quickly, he slid back across the bar back into the dining room.

Tom led Drew out of the Dining room and down a short hall. Nerves up, they examined small offices that stood off to the right. Finding nothing of use but a bottle of Ambien, some batteries and a quality bottle of single malt (someone's housewarming present) they continued to a common's room at the end of the hallway.

Done in a cliché nautical theme, the room was large with high whitewashed walls and ceilings. Several separate sitting areas with white wicker loveseats and distressed wooden coffee tables delineated different spaces for social banter. Sepia sailing pictures covered the walls and flags dangled from the exposed roof beams above. At the end of the room, the centerpiece, there was an enormous flat screen TV above a fireplace. On a shelf beside it were rows of DVDs and video games. Drew's spirits were lifted with this find.

"A little while back I made someone a promise I would like to keep," Drew said, crossing the room.

That's when the barking began. Drew froze and looked at Tom. The barking was growing louder.

"Oh Fuck," Drew said.

"OUT, NOW!" Tom directed, making haste down the hallway and back into the dining room.

Air horn blast one.

Now two.

Gunshots.

"Fuck."

More barking.

"Daryl," Drew called, charging after Tom, down the stairs and out into the parking lot.

There were two Akitas, running down the bridge toward Daryl. Shotgun raised, the first one leapt, foam dripping from its exposed teeth and gums as Daryl downed it with a pull of the trigger.

Without a single thought, Drew raised his .45 and the barking of the second dog cut was short as the large caliber round punched a hole into its neck. It lay on the ground, tried to take another breath and then its chest fell still.

Off in the distance, Drew could see the attention all of the commotion had drawn, Drinkers, leading the pack and closing ground quickly.

"We gotta move," Daryl said, taking the lead across the parking lot back to the marina dock. Once everyone was on the boardwalk, Tom slammed the coded gate shut.

"This isn't gonna hold the impact, keep going!" Tom barked.

Drew could see the first group of Drinkers entering the parking lot now, a wave of straggling Walkers followed behind, lumbering down the bridge. While their group rushed back to the *Twist*, Shark was busy starting the engines and put his hands up.

"What the fuck fellas?" he shouted as the trio climbed aboard.

Drew was last in the boat when the mass of bodies slammed into the gate at the top of the boardwalk. They went right over it and raced out onto the piers as Shark steered the boat into the waterway.

"What the fuck was up with those dogs, Daryl?" Tom asked, collapsing back into the *Twist*'s white vinyl seats.

"How should I know? I was just watching from the end of the bridge and saw movement. I didn't think anything of it as soon as I saw that it was just dogs. Then they just started barking and hauled ass across the bridge after they spotted me. Glad you guys heard the signal."

"Yes, thank you," Drew said. "They are probably running out of easy resources. That is my only guess. Rose and I saw three of them taking out Walkers the other night, just outside the fort."

"Shit, well I'm about ready to call it a day if you guys are," Daryl said.

"Well, you know if we do go back now Drew, Major Nate will want you and me on the wall tonight," Shark explained.

"Well, even still, if Daryl's had it, I have no problem heading back. I feel like today was kind of a bust anyway and it doesn't look like this weather is going to clear." Drew conceded.

Drew lay in his bunk but couldn't sleep. Shark in the bunk next to him snored deeply after finishing off half of the bottle of single malt they'd found in the clubhouse while on the ride back to the fort. He had been out since the second his back hit the pine straw mattress.

It was mid-afternoon and they needed rest if they were going to watch the wall that night but Drew couldn't slow his mind down. He felt like he had been living the last couple of days in a fog, a haze, as if his brain was using some self-preservation tactic to turn his reality into a dream state in order to soften the blow. Images of the woman's sunken face illuminated by penlight were playing out in his memory. How many survivors were out there? How many about to suffer in the same way as the woman in the walk in. What had she been surviving for? Surviving under those conditions at that. What were any of them surviving for?

It all just seemed like a roll of the dice. Some people won, some people lost, and it appeared the whole planet had been stuck playing this twisted game. Given the situation you were in when this nightmare started, it was nothing but a black or white outcome in the end. If you were held up in a fort surrounded by ocean and a sliver of land with unlimited food, fresh water, and even electricity-you ended up doing pretty well. If you lacked even one of life's basic necessities in this situation-you were hosed, plain and simple.

They had all of the resources, but the most important one of all had been to be part of a group. To be alone in this situation-the omega man-would have been like losing one of life's basic necessities, not survivable. The madness would set in. Hell, he was already beginning to feel it working its way into the leaky seal that retained his mental health. If it weren't for guys like the sleeping fool next to him, he would be the one drinking his own piss from the floor.

What was Shark's reason for hanging on? Did he have one? That was just it. Everyone had come together and had gone on living despite massive losses, just like that. They had survived physically and they had survived mentally, because of each other.

But what direction were they in? Where was the group headed? That was the secret that everyone kept inside but nobody spoke of-there was no direction. They were rudderless. Drew feared that once that moved from people's heads to people's lips, things may start to break down.

Major Nate had been a natural leader thus far. He understood that giving out tasks and providing direction led to order and wellbeing-but they were going to need more, a true light at the end of the tunnel.

Drew thought of Billy Jameson and Heidi, his cellmate and the conversation the group had about their demise. How long until this actually is over? Would those things survive in the summer? In Florida? In this humidity? Surely not, he hoped, but then that left those that were trapped inside buildings and other protected areas. There would always be hellish surprises around every corner. Disturbing as their prison experiment was, Drew understood its purpose. It was part of this hope. That was what everyone was looking for. What they were surviving for.

Once that finally came would the group stay together? Would they remain here? Living in their little medieval village? Or would they choose to set up shop down at the Ritz-Carlton with their 400 thread count sheets?

"One day at a time," I guess as the alcoholics put it. That is all they had for now. This was purgatory. It was wait time. Wait this out, stay secure, stay supplied.

He couldn't think about this anymore. He needed rest.

He thought of his son and a trick he had taught him to fall asleep when you just couldn't. Drew closed his eyes and he began thinking of random words: Car, blue, zebra, carpet, spoon, chocolate, bagpipes. He continued on and was soon asleep.

Chapter 19

Drew woke with a nudge of Shark's brogan pressing against his shoulder.

"It's 11:00. Get your ass up and eat this," Shark said, holding out a tin plate of crab cakes, green beans, and biscuits. "Crystal would have my ass if she knew I let this get cold. She stayed up late to make sure it wasn't. The beans are canned but she put something in them and shit, if you didn't think you were at the mutherfucking Ritz-Carlton."

"I appreciate it Shark," Drew said sitting up and taking the plate.

He handed Drew a warm can of Coke, "Here you go mate, sorry it's not a hot-toddie. The temperature has dropped again and that means you're gonna need your overcoat, and of course, it's still fucking raining outside," he said, looking over at the drizzle beading on the windows.

"Shit, of course it is. So who is at the gate tonight?" Drew asked.

"Pretty sure it's Faulkner. It only makes sense. He's practically moved into the com room now. It's right there at the entrance so he can have watch every night for all I care.

He doesn't seem to do much else anyway but hold up in there and play with his toys," Shark returned, shoving a biscuit in his mouth and chasing it with beer. He inhaled deeply, held it and let out an earth-shattering belch.

"You're something else," Drew said, shaking his head. "The college roommate I never had."

"Well, class is about to start. Finish that up cause we got to get a move on," Shark continued impatiently, "Max and Jeff have been out there walking the wall since this afternoon."

Drew followed Shark out into the night. The light drizzle turned out to be annoying but not intolerable and it had gotten quite a bit colder as he could now see his breath.

Most everyone had turned in for the night, but Drew could see that there was still light on in Crystal's kitchen, the flames flickering from the remnants of the fireplace.

They were on battery power at night so lights were kept to a minimum, only illuminating the tunnels to the bastions, outer walls and more importantly the latrine. The main buildings all had power but everyone kept in agreement with the required conservation. The structures remained only lit by fireplace light, giving all their windows a shimmering, golden glow-eyes of jack-o-lanterns.

They made their way up the western ramp up onto the terreplein of the wall and began their clockwise patrol. Just outside they looked out over the dunes to where the infected insomniac shadows loitered amongst clumps of sea oats.

"I gotta ask," Drew said.

"What's that bro?" Shark responded.

"All this," Drew said nodding in the direction of the monsters over the wall. "What is our purpose here?"

"Our Purpose? Purpose for life? Is that what you're

asking? Ha, ha, are you trying to get all philosophical on me?" Shark chuckled, "seriously?"

"C'mon tough guy, what do you think?" Drew asked again, feeling like Shark was brushing him off.

"How about this, I will tell you by the time we reach the northern bastion.

The two remained silent as they continued along the wall. In the distance, the clouds over the ocean flashed with lightning veins but were so distant that they rendered no report other than a faint rumble. Through the mist, the wreck of the Carnival *Fascination* off Cumberland was a dark mass that continued to block the horizon to the north. When they reached the northern bastion, Drew turned to Shark, "So, you gonna tell me?"

"Ok, my purpose? Our purpose? I don't know about everybody else but my purpose is to stay alive. Not that being alive in all of this is better than being dead. It is just that I know what alive is. It is being dead that I am unsure of," he paused. "Look, I'm not into the god thing, not at all, and religion says there is a place for people like me, unbelievers. Is that place worse than what is on the other side of this wall? I don't know but am not interested in finding out. Now if death brings nothingness? Maybe that would be better, but suicide for me is not an option because I am a player and players see how things pan out."

Drew responded with a smile. It was a typical Shark answer.

"What we should worry about is if all this is in vain. What if the world as we created it can't sustain with us being gone?" Shark continued.

"What do you mean?" Drew asked.

"People. You remember that BP thing. They spilled all that oil into the gulf. It took months to stop the flow. Those things could be happening all over the place with no one around to stop them. It takes people to fix problems like that. Mother Nature may not be able to handle them on her own. This infection may have been just…" Shark started, but was cut short by a loud bang that echoed out across the parade ground.

A single muffled bark came from the top of the infirmary/sundries building.

"What the fuck?" Drew said.

They both turned toward the front gate.

The darkened tunnel at the front sallyport boomed again.

"Is that the swingbri…?" Shark stopped midsentence as Drew and he watched a figure dart out of the tunnel and make a left into the prison, slamming the door shut behind him.

They both froze.

"That was Faulkner, holy fuck, that cocksucker let them in," Shark yelled. "Rose!"

She was already on it.

From her room on the upper floor of the infirmary/sundries building, the sound that they had all dreaded penetrated the night. Clang, clang, clang, clang!

Gunshots rang out next as the infected began to stream out onto the parade ground.

Lights in the surrounding buildings came on almost in unison. As soon as people saw what was going on they were darkened again.

As rigged, the stairs on the infirmary/sundries building fell away and crashed on the ground into a pile of lumber.

The plan had always been a safeguard in case of a small trickle, a breach in the wall somehow, not a full scale infiltration through the main gate. With the drawbridge secure in combination with the gate, the place had been impenetrable from the outside. They had never considered the danger might be from within. There would be no way to stop the flow.

Gunshots from the window of the infirmary/sundries building continued to roll off one by one and Drinkers began to fall as they entered from the sallyport tunnel.

"That's my girl!" Shark yelled.

Drew snapped into action, "Shark, head around to the east bastion, I will take the south. We can't let them make it up the ramps onto the walls, we need to flank them and pile them up. Pile them up so in front so that no more can get in," he barked. "Go!"

Just then the wall behind them burst into clouds of orange mist from exploding brick. In their excitement the sound of approaching boats had gone unnoticed.

They spun around.

From what Drew could tell, it was two US coast guard boats with .50 caliber machine guns. They were headed in the direction of the fort chewing the top of the wall with their forward guns.

"Run, get to your bastian!" Drew yelled, "There's no time."

Scurrying along the southwestern wall, Drew got a clear view of the main barracks where everyone was bunked. Muzzle flashes appeared in the windows upstairs but he couldn't see who was behind them. He knew Rose, Josh and Bella were ok on the top floor of the infirmary/sundries building, but didn't know about the barracks. Major Nate, Sergeant Sloan, and Colonel Wilcox had always been bunked in private rooms adjacent the enlisted bunkroom on the bottom floor where Drew roomed with Shark, Tom, Carey, and Max. Elizabeth and Jeff were up on the top floor in separate private officer's quarters along with Daryl (who had since moved in with Crystal) and the yankees, Sam and Martha Appleman. Jason Freeman had taken up residence in his blacksmith shop and should be protected by the iron bars on the windows.

From his position, he saw the Drinkers enter the door to his room on the bottom floor of the barracks. A chair exploded out of window on the adjacent wall of the building and Max and Tom dove out behind it.

"Get to the balcony above," Drew yelled out, watching Max try and give Tom a boost up. It was too high.

Just then, the door to the blacksmith shop opened and Jason emerged firing shots with a pistol into the crowd of Drinkers that were coming around the side of the building.

"Get the fuck in here," Drew heard Jason scream.

Tom turned and followed him through the open door.

Max tried to crowd in behind but was too late, one of the Drinker's grabbed hold of his blouse and pulled him back through the doorway. Slinging him to the ground, the drinker reared back and dove onto him.

"Mother fucker," Drew yelled, firing his .45 wildly into the pulsating mob of infected that immediately engulfed Max. He had not made a sound the entire time.

Drew put his radio to his mouth and yelled into it, "Whoever is in the barracks, take those fuckers out at the entrance, pile them up at the front so no more can get in."

The shots from the Coast Guard .50 calibers ceased and Drew looked back toward their direction. He heard voices, yelling, it sounded like Spanish.

What the fuck is going on? Drew thought to himself, crossing from the terraplein to the top of the outer wall at the latrines and across to the southern bastion.

Drew was relieved to find that the staircase door was already shut and there was a rifle with several hundred rounds of ammunition stored there as Major Nate had suggested.

Drew heard a man's screams coming from the latrines. Who was it? Fuck, fuck, fuck.

He had to stay on task and watch the ramp while trying to take the infected out on the swing bridge.

From across the way, he could see that Shark had already taken his post, muzzle flashes already appearing from his direction.

He focused on the swing bridge and began firing.

The piling fallen bodies on the bridge were slowing them down but the Drinkers were making their way over the growing mound.

Drew could see that Jeff had already spread the word and the muzzle flashes out the barracks window were all aimed at the front entrance. Blocking his view of the infirmary/sundries building he could only hear the sound of Rose's bolt action .30-06 cracking off at regular intervals.

Drew looked down at his radio and thought to request out a status update when he heard gunshots coming from the area around the southwest bastion. Men, he counted at least eight of them, were running down the terraplein in his direction.

Grabbing his radio, "Barracks, cease fire, bad men approaching your 6 o'clock."

There was no response and the muzzle flashes continued from the building.

As the men continued toward him they didn't seem at all interested in the barracks as they jogged past with a steely purpose. Casually, one of them stopped, lit a Molotov cocktail and threw it against the upper floor balcony and continued on with the group toward Drew's position.

Drew kept his head down as they passed his location and made their way around the top of the wall above the entrance to the fort.

"Shark, cease fire, men approaching, don't give up your location. Rose, cease fire until I command."

Rose and Shark heard him and acknowledged by going silent.

The barracks continued to pump lead at the horde below while Drew could see that Martha and Jeff were scrambling to put out the fire, burning on the balcony.

Peeping up from the shadows of the south bastion, Drew could see that there were actually nine men. They were fully armed with pistols, automatic rifles, and were wearing backpacks. They were dark skinned and dressed in battered clothes and continued to yell in Spanish back and forth. They disputed something for a minute and then three of them hurled backpacks over the wall down onto the swing bridge.

"Rose, Shark, dead ahead at your 12, men above the front entrance. On my mark, take your shots and make them clean, over," Drew radioed.

One of the men held a radio to his mouth and was screaming more Spanish into it. Not understanding a word of it, Drew lined him up in his sights.

"Alright, now!" Drew radioed out.

In unison, three of the nine silhouettes dropped to the ground. Before anyone could line up another shot, the six remaining men dispersed as a massive explosion erupted from the front of the fort in a tremendous ball of fire.

Drew could feel the heat immediately as the temperature of the air jumped 50 degrees.

When the debris settled, he didn't have a location on the men anymore, his ears were ringing and his head felt like it was full of cotton. Looking through the clearing smoke he saw that the bridge was devastated and a large section of the brick front archway had collapsed.

Those men wanted the fort.

Gunfire had now ceased in the barracks and it looked like all hands were on deck trying to put out the spreading fire on the balcony.

Drew felt helpless.

His radio popped to life.

Gunshots started ringing out again.

"Drew, I got these fuckers over on my side now. All six of them, I'm pinned down but they don't seem to know I'm up here. They are taking out the infected and trying to clear the east ramp, over," Shark said.

Drew heard a single, telltale shot from the .30-06. "One more down, Drew. Rose took him out," Shark came again. Gunshots suddenly erupted as Drew could now see the men on the northeastern wall lighting up Rose's location on the top floor of the infirmary/sundries.

"…shit, Drew they are really on her," Shark came across.

"Rose! Report your status…" Drew radioed out.

There was nothing but silence from the infirmary/sundries except for Bella's frantic barking from the top floor.

The .30-06 rang out again.

"She has moved to another window, took out another one," Shark said.

"Rose, cease fire, play dead!" Drew radioed.

Drew could see that the temporary distraction that Rose had caused allowed the Drinkers to dial in on the remaining men's location. There must have been over 400 infected roaming the inner grounds now and their ranks quickly turned their attention to the east ramp.

The thick mob began their ascent when one of the men hurled a backpack into the horde. The explosion came and lay the infected down like a crop circle.

Again, "Rose, gimme your status, over," Drew pleaded across the VHF.

Still, no response.

"Shit."

"Shark, I'm headed around your way oceanside, gonna try to pin them in while they are preoccupied with the freaks. How are you doing on ammo?"

"Just under hundred rounds for the rifle, your Glock 19 is already out cause I had to use it coming up the stairwell, over." Shark returned. "What's the status of the barracks? I'm seeing lots of smoke from where I am."

Drew was back on the outer wall headed to the southwest bastion. As he passed the barracks he could see that Jeff and Martha were getting things pretty much under control.

"It should be alright, the rain may be helping their situation. Could have been worse. They coulda thrown one of those backpacks, over."

"Looks like they are saving those for the infected," Shark said.

Just then, another explosion rocked a mass of the reassembled freaks on the ramp.

The infected were beginning to take notice of Drew and followed his progress on either side as he made his way across the top of the outer wall over to the southwest bastion.

As he approached, he could already see that the entrance

to the spiral stairwell leading to the top was open and gun drawn, he put a round through the first Drinkers head that emerged from the darkness. The body fell lifelessly back onto others that were trying to make their way to the top.

Drew slammed Jason's grate shut and locked it.

The infected had made it onto the top of the terreplein via the western ramp. From here on Drew would have to continue on via the top of the three foot wide outer wall.

Drew unloaded the rest of the rounds in his rifle into the infected that were swarming the barracks and exchanged the weapon for a shotgun stored at the top of the bastion.

Catching his breath, he continued out onto the wall that lead over to the northwest bastion. Careful not to slip on the wet, narrow brick ledge, he passed the knotted ropes the men had used to come over the wall. He looked out over Cumberland Sound where two hundred yards out he could see a go-fast boat idling against the current. He was able to keep low and avoid being seen just before he reached the next bastion.

Gunshots rang out and rounds struck the wall at his feet just as he crossed over the wall into the bastion.

There was a burning sensation in his leg. Jerking up his pant leg, he noticed a round had gone through his uniform pants and grazed his calf.

As it had done the previous day, blood flowed steadily into his socks.

"You fucker," he cursed, knowing it could have been much worse.

Drew pumped a few rounds in the direction of the boat and it responded by increasing the distance between them.

The sound of his 12 gauge alerted the four remaining men who had huddled alongside a large concrete blockade next to the defunct eastern cannon battery.

Another flurry of Spanish echoed out across the empty space. He didn't understand anything they were saying but it did have a panicky tone to it.

Two men broke from the group and made their way in his direction, using the cannons as shelter as they advanced toward Drew's location.

"That's right my man, lead them away from me," Shark came across on the radio. "I have a shot if you can continue to draw them."

Another backpack explosion went off on the ramp again, keeping the infected at bay. A single shot echoed out from Shark's position and Drew saw the man who threw the backpack drop to the ground.

Three left.

One of the men stepped out and immediately unloaded an automatic weapon at Shark's stronghold. A blast came from a side window of Rose's building as she immediately took him out.

The remaining two men came out into the open, firing wildly and continued to approach Drew's location.

There wasn't anywhere else for them to go. They had thrown the last of the backpacks already and the horde had made its way up onto the rampart.

Drew slumped down behind the wall and waited until their screams in Spanish called out as the Drinker's made contact with their prey. Drew checked his wounded leg again and picked up the radio. "Shark, Rose, start taking out the infected. Those men are down but this isn't over."

"Alright, Drew I'm headed around to the front entrance to make sure no more are getting through. Start making your way to the barracks and see how the others are making out, over." Shark replied.

"Roger that," Drew confirmed.

Climbing back onto the outer wall, Drew began to work his way counterclockwise back to the barracks. He kept careful watch out over Cumberland Sound and the boat that hung offshore.

Careful that the recoil didn't knock him over the wall, he pumped 12 gauge rounds into the reaching infected below. The backpack bombs had reduced the numbers immensely but the infected had covered the entire grounds and Drew had no idea how far they had worked themselves into the seams of the infrastructure.

The bell clanged again from the sundries building and Drew froze in immediate panic from the sound of it.

What the fuck now?, he thought, but quickly realized what was happening. The infected, minus the ones below him were responding to the sound and began to migrate back out to the parade ground.

"Good girl, Rose, keep after it," he said to himself. He was also relieved that it probably meant Rose and Josh were alright.

Bella's continued yelping assured him that his Little Gremlin was up still up there with them, alive and well.

He finally arrived back at the southwest bastion. From his new position, he could see the Shark's dark shadow as he was making his way along the outer wall from the east bastion to the damaged front entrance.

The roof of the sallyport cut through the terreplein here and was the only other place where it conjoined with the outer wall (the wall dividing up the latrine being the other). The infected had taken this route and made their way out onto the wall but many were losing their balance and falling to either side. Those that did not were met by muzzle fire from Shark's rifle.

Drew could also see that the two doors on the bottom floor of the barracks were smashed in. They had marked the entrance to the private rooms of the regimental staff, Sergeant Bill, Major Nate and the Colonel Wilcox. Unless they had been in some other area of the fort during all of this, things didn't look good.

Drew felt sadness and anger boiling up in him and he fought to choke it back.

To the right, Drew could see that the second floor balcony had collapsed extinguishing the rest of the fire as the embers from the burning structure fought against the rain to stay alive.

Once more, gunfire burst forth from the barracks second floor out onto the parade ground where the horde was gathering. Drew could account for some of the survivors on the top floor. There were only three definites.

"Martha, Jeff, Elizabeth," he called out, between bursts of gunfire.

Jeff came to the one of the doorways that led out to where the balcony once had been.

"How many people are with you up there?" Drew called out.

"Just my mom and Mrs. Appleman," he returned.

"Keep after it," Drew called out, waving him back inside. Where the fuck was everyone else? Daryl? Crystal? Buddy parks?

Mr. Appleman?

Jeff's presence had attracted a group of infected that were on the terreplein and had walked out onto the metal roof of the blacksmith shop. It was bowing in dramatically with their combined weight. Drew took them down quickly fearing that they would collapse down inside where Jason and Tom were holding up.

The numbers of infected were clearly thinning now as the parade deck reminded Drew of the aerial shots he had seen of the Jonestown massacre with civilian followers strewn across their encampment. From what he could tell the Drinkers were all finished off at this point. They were the most dangerous but ultimately first to go because they literally ran right into your gunfire like flies into a zapper.

Drew crossed over the tops of the latrine wall feeling comfortable enough again to be on the earthen terreplein.

His radio popped to life.

"Front entrance is wasted. We are buttoned back up securely though, over," Shark reported.

"Roger that, over," he returned and made his way toward Sharks location, keeping close eye on the western ramp that lead down to the parade ground. There were now only around 50 stragglers working their way out onto the open field and Elizabeth, Jeff, and Rose were taking care of them.

Drew could see Shark crossing from the wall over to the parapet, clearing more stragglers that fought to climb the sandy ramparts after him.

Noticing the burn in his leg more now, Drew winced as he approached Shark.

"You ok?" Shark asked.

"I will be fine," Drew responded, "we are gonna have to sweep this whole place out. Tom and Jason are in the blacksmith shop…"

Shark wasn't listening. He stared through him.

"What's up?" Drew asked.

In all the excitement, Shark had forgotten about the man who started this. His mind snapped clear again, "Faulkner, that sonovabitch!" he screamed.

Changing out a fresh magazine in his rifle, Shark sprinted along the wall and down the ramp to the parade ground, taking out approaching stragglers. Drew was at his heels, as they approached the guardroom.

"Yo, keep your cool," Drew called out after him.

Either Shark didn't hear him or wasn't listening. He grabbed the front door of the sealed room and wrenched at it but it wouldn't budge.

Faulkner had locked himself in from the inside.

"Hey Faulkner, you fuck," Shark screamed, rearing back the butt of his rifle and smashing in the glass windows from between the wrought iron bars. "What did you do? You fuck."

It was dark inside but Drew could see that Guy Faulkner was sitting at a wooden table facing them with his head down. It remained down when he spoke.

"They have my wife."

"Look at me you cocksucker, who has your wife? Who were those men?" Shark demanded, smashing at the window again.

"Pirates, I–I–don't know where they are from." He spoke slowly and his voice was cracking.

"Pirates? You're a fucking madman," Shark said, growing more enraged with every answer, "Who did this and don't say pirates again or I'm gonna take the top of your head off."

"His name is Carlos, he was the one in charge, he took my wife. They said that they were going to kill her if I didn't help them take the fort."

"And so you did, and that's the deal with all your fucking radio getup-to make contact with them. Speak you fuck! I'm right, aren't I?" Shark came again. "Your wife is fucking dead by the way. I'm sure of it you fucking fool!"

Faulkner remained with his head down. Drew saw that he was weeping now.

Gunshots rang in the distance from the barracks, as straggling Walkers approached the conversation taking place. They were quickly dropped to the ground, joining the mass of corpses that lay scattered about.

Shark turned and started running across the parade ground, toward the northern wall.

"Shark!" Drew called out, chasing after him. "Where the hell are you going?"

Shark stopped and turned, "to get this Carlos fuck."

"Shark, this isn't the time," Drew insisted, but Shark wasn't having any of it.

"This is going down right now, and when I get back, that fuck in the guardroom is mine Drew, understand?"

"I'm coming with you then," Drew said.

Around him the gunshots had ceased. People watched and listened from the windows of the two buildings.

"No, you are not Drew," Shark said, popping him in the chest with the palm of his hand. "Take care of them for me."

Out of the corner of his eye, Drew saw Rose cutting a path through the bodies. She was headed to the guardroom and paid no attention to Shark and Drew in the middle of the parade ground.

"Rose, wait, it isn't safe out here." Drew called out and made off in her direction. His head was spinning, tunneling his vision.

Rose continued across the parade ground with the weapon at her side. Approaching the window Shark had ventilated, she raised her rifle and fired a single shot into the darkness before Drew could bat the barrel away.

Faulkner crumpled to the floor.

Drew turned back to the parade ground. Shark was gone.

"Drew," Rose called, trying to get his attention. She racked another round in the chamber of the bolt action.

"Drew!" She screamed this time, trying to get him to break out of his zone.

Drew came back to earth and made eye contact with Rose who seemed to be in clearer focus than he had ever seen her. She was pressing forward and Mr. Faulkner's death was not even an afterthought. He could see it in her eyes as she stared into him.

"I saw it earlier from the window. Daryl and Crystal are in the cistern drain over near the kitchen. Buddy, he helped them inside and almost made it in himself but it was too late. Go help them," she ordered and made off toward the barracks in the direction of the regimental staff quarters.

Drew almost called out after her but watching her cross the parade ground with the rifle in the ready position, he turned and headed toward the kitchen.

His legs felt like they were going to buckle under him as he jogged between the body parts and chunks of debris from the bombed out ramp, careful that there were no infected with bite still left in them.

There were several drains around the parade grounds for collecting water. Heavy grates covered them and the space beneath offered sufficient room to conceal a person or in this case, two. A pile of body parts lifted and then fell back again as Drew approached and saw Daryl struggling with the heavy wooden grating. Drew cleared the top of it from the wreckage of the infected, as Daryl called up to him.

"Help me get this fucking thing open," he said.

"Are you guys ok?" Drew said, sliding the grate over to the side.

Crystal was crying and shaky but looked to be alright.

"Thanks man," Daryl said, taking Drew's hand and climbing out of the hole. "What the fuck happened here?" He continued, looking around at the surrounding destruction.

Drew put his hand down and helped Crystal out. Getting a good look around, she put her arms around Drew and buried her sobbing face into his chest.

"It's all over?" She asked.

"Keep your guard up but I think we got them all," Drew tried to calm her.

"Daryl and I were in the kitchen talking with Buddy when we heard the bridge and the gate open-then the bell. Buddy rushed us outside and held open the grate while we climbed down there. They got Buddy before he could climb inside. He saved our lives," Crystal said.

Drew looked at Daryl who had his back to him. He could see when he lifted his arm to his face he was doing so to wipe away tears.

From across the parade ground, a single muzzle flash

accompanied the sound of the .30-06 coming from Colonel Wilcox's room in the regimental staff's quarters. Rose appeared in the adjacent doorway, tossing the rifle aside.

"Josh, go back inside," she called out, as her brother climbed down from the infirmary/sundries building to investigate what had taken place. He ignored her and kept his pace in her direction.

Rose wouldn't let him through the doorway and Drew understood why.

"Rose, what happened in there?" he screamed, "Rose you tell me what happened in there!"

"Josh, go back to the infirmary." Rose said in a way that was barely audible from across the grounds.

Elizabeth and Jeff came around the right side of the building with Jason and Tom close behind.

"Josh, you are going to have to come with me," Elizabeth said, coming to Rose's assistance.

"I'm going in Rose!" Josh screamed, ignoring Elizabeth, "you can't stop me."

It was just then something inside of Drew, an aspect of his personality perhaps, stepped all the way through the door. It had been his advisor during this nightmare, but now it was giving all the orders, commanding Drew to take charge.

"Fix this!" it screamed in his head.

"Alright, I'm gonna need everyone at the flagpole. Now!" Drew called out, breaking from Crystal and jogging across the parade deck.

"Move people, flagpole, now!" he barked out again,

making a circling motion above his head with an index finger. His voice carried out like a drill sergeant. He was amazed to see people hustling over at his direction.

At the flagpole, they gathered around him.

"First of all, is everyone able to do the tasks that I am about to assign?"

Everyone stood and nodded.

"Ok, Tom, you and Jason arm yourselves and cover the wall starting with the front entrance and heading around to the north. We need to make sure this place is swept clean of all the infected and I want all evidence of this atrocity collected. We need to find out about this enemy. Stay alert in case there is some sort of follow up attack.

Elizabeth, Jeff and Daryl, I need you with me to cover every square inch of this place and after that I want every single one of these bodies dumped over the west wall. We will not spend a second night in a place that looks like this. The bodies of our loved ones will be placed inside the southwest bastion in wait before we have a proper burial for them here within the grounds. Ladies and gentlemen, they wouldn't want us to mourn them now if they knew how much work we have to do here.

Crystal, I'm going to have to ask you to do what you do best. People are going to need their energy.

Josh, your now promoted to Colonel. You will be taking over command from Colonel Wilcox. Return my salute and that makes it official," Drew said, saluting him.

Josh stood at attention and took the commission by returning it.

"Ok your first assignment once we clear this area is getting me a flag on this pole," Drew directed the boy, striking the metal pole with a clang.

Rose, I need you to find me something for this leg; it's not bad but needs to be wrapped up.

"Elizabeth, where is Mrs. Appleton?" Drew asked.

"She was right down behind us as we came out," Jeff answered instead. "I think she is out looking for her husband."

"Ok, go with your mom and Daryl and try and find her."

"We need get moving and get this done. Everyone knows that this is our lives and our security at stake here," Drew closed, and with that everyone took to their duties.

Elizabeth stayed back.

When everyone was at a good distance she asked, "Where is he Drew? I saw what happened in the courtyard. Where did he go?"

"Elizabeth, I need you to focus right now. Tomorrow morning when the sun comes out I will take Daryl and go after him."

"Promise me Drew. Promise me you will go looking for him," she pleaded.

"I promise you this this, I love him too and I won't stop looking until he is found."

When Rose was bandaging up Drew's leg she had told him what had happened inside the regimental staff's quarters and Jeff was the one to go inside the small rooms with Drew to collect the bodies of Major Nate, Sergent Sloan and Colonel Wilcox.

They found the Colonel still in his wheelchair with a single rifle shot through his head as Rose had been the one to set him free. A motionless drinker was at his feet. Having taken on the infection as a Walker, the Colonel had been able to bring one of them down before his own transformation.

Their bodies were brought, as Drew had instructed, to the southwest bastion and it wasn't long before the bodies of Buddy Parker, Max Dipace, Carey Douglas, Sam and Martha Appleman joined them side-by-side on the slate floor of the dark room.

Sadly, it was Elizabeth that had to be the one to put Martha Appleton down. She had been walking with Daryl when she heard screaming coming from the latrine. Everyone in the fort had in fact heard it.

Martha had found that her husband had been attacked while relieving himself. When Elizabeth arrived on scene, Martha was holding his dead body, pants still at his ankles. Elizabeth said that Martha was crying out for her husband when he just simply opened up his eyes, rose up, and bit a chunk out of the side of her cheek.

Elizabeth had to shoot both of them.

Drew joined Tom and Jason on the wall and they were able to recover the bodies of six of their nine attackers. Exhausted, they had been at it all night and the light was beginning to appear over the horizon through the haze as they inspected the bodies of the unknown enemies. They were laid out side by side next to the cannons on the terreplein of the eastern wall and they appeared as strangers, foreigners.

"Faulkner called them pirates," Drew said as the three of them stood over the broken bodies of their dark skinned invaders.

"Think they are Cuban?" Tom asked.

"I'm not sure, maybe South American? There are know pirates in the Gulf of Mexico area. I read about them on the ICC-CCS website when I was preparing for my trip," Drew paused. "As opportunists, it would make sense for them to migrate north with all this going on."

"There must be easy picking out there, that's for sure. Those are fucking US Coast Guard boats they came in on," Jason added, digging through the pants pockets of one of them. "I'm not finding any identification, wallets, or anything on them. Just cigarettes, keys to the boats, and-hey check it out, the tattoos here." Jason tore back the tattered black button down shirt one of them was wearing, exposing his chest.

"Columbians," Tom said, immediately spotting an inked yellow, blue, and red striped flag of the country. The bottom red stripe of the flag was detailed to make it look like it was dripping blood.

"They may be cartel. Looks like some of them have the same tats. "They're not carrying anything worries me though, must mean they have been holed up pretty close to here. A neighboring island maybe. They sure weren't packed for a long haul," Drew said. "There was a speedboat just off the coast during the attack. I could only see one person aboard and I'm pretty sure that Shark went after him. You would think that if there were any more of these guys, then they would have joined in on tonight's little raid. That being said, I believe that we are safe at least for now but we need to provision the bastions again with weapons, and ammo, and keep someone on guard along the seaward walls at all times," Drew said, spotting Daryl coming up to them on the pockmarked eastern ramp.

"Yo Drew we got to bounce," he called out, "We got a Shark to catch and Elizabeth is already on my ass about it."

Drew looked out over the water, over to Faulkner's catamaran and the two Coastguard boats beached next to it.

"Alright. Jason, hand me those keys."

Chapter 20

"Where did he go?" Drew asked Bella, who was zipped up securely in his uniform blouse, leaving nothing exposed but her little head.

He was trying to play out possible scenerios in his head while he fired up the twin outboards on one of the 25 foot coast guard port security boats. The seas the night before had been pretty churned up so it was most likely that Shark headed inland, but north to Cumberland, or south, behind Amelia? That was the question.

"Drew, let's focus on Amelia for now. We got a lot of ground to cover. Shark shoulda been back by now one way or the other and the best choice for him would have been Amelia," Daryl said. He picked up the radio and called out on 16. "Yo Shark, this is Daryl, gimme your 20, over."

There was no response.

Daryl scanned the coastline of Amelia with Drew's battered green binoculars as they headed toward downtown. They made a right toward Oyster Bay and followed the inlet into the marina. There were no more infected around and there was no sign of Shark.

Crossing over to the Fernandina Beach City Marina area, they guided the boat between the rows of docks looking for the black hull of the *Twist*. Drew felt like jumping behind the .50 cal and mowing down the infected that ran down the docks to greet them. Bella vibrated against his chest as she growled with apprehension.

Finding nothing, they made their way back to the Amelia Island Yacht Basin where Shark had rescued him from the bird shit waitress. Thinking about it again made the hairs stand up on the back of his neck and caused him to worry for Shark even more. Interestingly enough, the place was still very quiet. There was only a single Walker, a young female in a green Applebee's uniform standing in the road that lead out to the bridge. She was more interested in the squirrel on a tree branch above her head than their passing boat.

As they cruised along, Daryl remained silent as Drew explained in more detail how the events of that night had played out. He told of the ringing bell, the coast guard boats, and the men running along the western wall. He told of how Rose had ended up taking most of the bomb throwing pirates out with her rifle as well as ending Guy Faulkner who had compromised the fort because of a captive wife. He also filled him in on the man named "Carlos," the one who Shark had probably been after. When he concluded they both remained silent and exchanged very few words-both lost in thought. Drew could tell that Daryl was as exhausted as he was. He could see it on his face, the confusion, the sadness, and the overall grief over what had happened and what they were now doing, out there looking for their closest partner after already so many losses.

As they headed south away from the Yacht Basin and through the pilings of the Shave Bridge, Daryl broke the silence. "I gotta say I'm feeling guilty, man."

"Why do you say that?" Drew asked.

"For not being out there with you guys, for being stuck in that fucking hole, man."

"I told you again how it played out, Daryl, there was nothing that you could have done from where you were when this whole thing broke out. You are not in any hole, and right now, the way I see it, you are in this shit with the rest of us and that's where I need you." Drew explained.

"I know, I just also keep thinking about Buddy, he was so close to making it and then was just gone," Daryl said, as a tear came down his cheek. He didn't care anymore so he didn't wipe it away.

He put the VHF to his mouth.

"Shark, this is Daryl, I need you to talk to me, over."

There was still silence over the VHF as they pressed on through where the waterway forked, keeping left of the red channel markers that lead them toward the south end of the island.

"Our boy Shark is something else ain't he?" Daryl said, trying to lighten things up.

"Yes, he is." Drew agreed, continuing south and searching the marsh to either side of them. In the distance, they could make out the southern bridge—and they approached.

Suddenly, they thought they heard multiple gunshots off to port.

Drew slowed the boat trying to quiet the motors so they could hear more clearly as they scanned the docks along the coastline. The houses that they led to were quite a distance through the marsh over boardwalks that were populated with infected. As was their nature, they were coming down in response to the passing boat.

"Drew, fuck man there she is," Daryl yelled out in alarm, pointing out to the pair of bridges.

Drew saw her too; the familiar black hull was apparently wedged within the pilings of the main bridge.

"Hand me the radio," Drew said, taking it from Daryl.

"*Twist of Fate*, this is Drew, do you copy?"

There was still no return from the radio as they sped toward the crippled vessel.

As they made their approach, Daryl took the radio again.

"Shark, we are nearing the *Twist* and it looks like you may have gotten pretty messed up. We heard the gunshots but we are not sure of your position, come back, channel 1-6."

There was still no response on the VHF.

The *Twist*'s wreckage sent a panic through Drew. She had been impaled on a piece of the airplane debris that was hung up in the span and looked as if she would sink immediately.

Drew investigated and it looked like she had been scavenged for supplies but he was discouraged at the brown, bloodstained water that sloshed around in the submerged stern.

It was heartbreaking.

Above them, the infected looked down mocking them with their croaks and hissing, not revealing the secrets of what had happened there hours ago.

Drew headed back over to the docks where the gunshots had sounded out. All that filled the air now was more croaking of Drinkers that had now crowded onto the platforms at the end of the boardwalks.

Daryl looked at Drew with a look of dismay as they circled again.

"What do you think?" Drew asked him.

"What I think is that I heard gunshots. Now, I'm seeing the infected but nobody's shooting anymore. To me that's not a good sign."

"Maybe the one shooting wasn't Shark." Drew said. "Maybe it is another survivor, or group of survivors up where those houses are," he continued, pointing.

"Well, from the looks of things there isn't much we can do here. Not with all those freaks blocking our way that is. Your right, it probably was another survivor. Shark could have never made it up that length of pier through all those Drinkers. Guns or not," Daryl pointed out.

Drew nodded in agreement and they headed out through the bridges and southward around the eastern coast of Little Talbot island. The tide had been going out about the time Shark would have hit the bridge. Drew figured his only route off the vessel would be by sea so he could have been washed out.

They continued through the rough waters of the Atlantic side of the island. Off to starboard was a long stretch of beach with a large horde of infected that gathered around a wooden ramp sloping up to a beach access. Drew could tell that Daryl was also searching the infected to see if Shark was perhaps wandering aimlessly amongst them. He didn't mention it though.

"Hey, looks like we may be getting low on gas, this thing is pretty thirsty. We are gonna need to head back soon," Drew said.

"Yeah, let's go ahead and do that. I know it's rough but let's take the Atlantic side back and see what we can see."

Drew spun the Coast Guard boat around. The sky was still grey and the ocean was white capping. Drew stayed as close to shore as he could safely manage as they headed north back to the fort, continuing to see if they recognized any of the infected coming down to the beach to meet them. Neither of them wanted to say what was on their minds.

Shark was probably never going to be seen again.

✣ ✣ ✣

The small 25 foot security boat struggled in the rough seas just offshore of the Ritz-Carlton hotel when Drew radioed out to them.

"Ritz-Carlton Hotel, this is Drew Mcfarland of the Fort Clinch survivors, over."

The VHF remained silent.

Daryl scanned the top of the hotel with the binoculars as Drew fought the current.

"Drew, I'm not seeing anything. Maybe they got overtaken. The place actually looks pretty shot up," Daryl said, handing the binoculars over to Drew.

Drew scanned the building and noted the place was now riddled with pockmarks from heavy caliber fire. A number of the glass doors were shattered and the dead slumped over balcony railings along the buildings ocean side. There was no sign of movement on the roof and no one came out on the balconies of the top floor.

"It wasn't like this when we were here before," Drew said.

"Ritz-Carlton Hotel, this is Drew Mcfarland of the Fort Clinch survivors, over," Drew radioed again but his calls were not returned.

"Fuck it," he said, heading the boat north again, back to the Fort.

When their coast guard vessel beached back into the soft white sand at the fort, what was left of the small band of survivors were standing there, waiting for their return.

In the distance, off near the western wall, a large greasy plume of smoke swirled and spun, rising high into the air in a thick column. Clearly, they had been continuing the cleanup process and were now disposing of the bodies, setting them alight just behind the latrines. They all looked like they had been working in a slaughterhouse.

Drew looked out at the haggard expressions of his pathetic group. He had radioed ahead to Tom already and had given him a brief synopsis of their trip around the island but they were gathered there as a group to hear the details in person.

Drew and Daryl offered their theories on Shark and the *Twist of Fate* and how they had heard gunshots before finding the abandoned vessel. They told them of the salvaged provisions aboard and about the bloodstained decks of the boat. They finally concluded with the Ritz-Carlton radio attempt and the lack of response from them, as well as the condition of the building as they had found it now.

The group stood silent as they took the news.

Drew felt it hard to speak at times, especially with Elizabeth looking at him with the expression on her face of anger, loss, and overall abandonment. She was the first to speak out.

"Drew, look," she began calmly, but Drew cut her off.

"Elizabeth, I know what you're going to say and I promise we will keep looking for him. We can't give up hope despite our findings today. You people have become my family and Shark was a very important member of that. I feel that it is my duty and obligation to pursue the search for him as I would any one of you."

"Drew," Tom interrupted him. "You don't have to say anything more. What you did last night is the reason that we are all still standing here. I think what Elizabeth was about to say was thank you. We all thank you for what you have done. We have all been talking and with your acceptance we request that you take over the fort's command from Major Nate."

Elizabeth spoke, "It was your leadership that got us through this and it is the same leadership that we need to hold this place together. Please accept the responsibility."

Drew looked around at the seven faces staring back at him for more answers.

"Does she speak for all of you?" Drew asked them.

"She does, Drew," Tom said, as the other survivors nodded in unison.

Chapter 21

Now officially under new command, the group of nine survivors continued with the arduous task of removing corpses and adding them to the smoldering heap behind the latrines. Drew learned that Jason had been the one to get the fire started and had done so with the body of Guy Faulkner, simply dousing it in lamp oil and heaving over the wall. There had been no ceremony or remorse but only just a part of the exhaustive work that they all struggled to put behind them.

Drew was pleased, but it didn't surprise him that despite the heavy atmosphere, people were moving, making things happen, and pressing on. It was that drive and attitude that had brought them all together here and it was that attitude that would be crucial to their recovery.

Just after sunset, the nine survivors gathered around the graves where they buried the bodies of their fallen next to Eileen Simmons.

Max, Carey. Buddy, Mr. and Mrs. Appleton, Sergeant

Bill, Major Nate, and Colonel Wilcox were finally no more and everyone said their peace. Drew was the last to speak.

"There was a day that each one of us had hopes and dreams. We looked at the world as organized, predictable, and secure, a place where there was possibility to build our own future, our own destiny. Anything we could hope for we could achieve if we put our hearts into it," Drew paused. "And then one day it just disappears. For me it was just a couple of years before any of this took place. Everything that I had expected out of life, despite my hard work, just vanished within an instant. I had no power over it, no say, and no control. I withdrew and cursed the world around me. I felt betrayed and let down. I lost trust and faith in everything around me. I was an empty shell and even when I thought that I may be getting on my feet I was knocked down again by this new situation. But this time though, it was different. Everyone around me was knocked down as well. What that reminded me of, was that in my suffering, I had never been alone. Mine was not an isolated incident. We all share the same pains, and grief, and sense of loss and disparity, but within these walls we do it together and together we can take our destiny back. We can wipe the slate clean and press on. Those that died last night, died believing in that dream; the dream of hope and a possible future, despite tremendous obstacles. They died for something that I didn't have when I arrived here to this family. Now I would die for the same. With everything you have in you I encourage you to rebuild your dreams. Plan for the future and look forward to it. Do it for yourselves and do it for the men and women that lie in the ground in front of us. Let us share each other's wishes and hopes, and come together to make them all a reality. Get some rest ladies and gentlemen and mourn the ones that we have lost tonight but save tomorrow as a day of celebration. We were victorious here and this place remains a place of hope and possibility. Tomorrow it is Thanksgiving and may it be a day of thanks." Drew paused and smiled, "And you know if Shark were here, he would insist on a block party."

After the makeshift ceremony everyone headed off to bed, but Drew doubted many were sleeping. Drew was up too, exhausted physically and mentally but unable to even close his eyes. It was going to be hard living like this now, walking down the long dark tunnels of the fort, climbing the circular bastian stairwells and even entering the communications room where Mr. Faulkner had taken such crucial part in their attack. Shadows danced in all the dark corners and the smell of death was all around. Through the slit windows the infected still reached and clutched, ever reminding you of what you could become.

Bella was with him as they climbed the staircase of the northwest bastian without the little Chihuahua sensing any danger. Drew knew there was none but having her along was comforting, nonetheless.

Again, he found himself staring out over the sea. It was much more visible tonight with the clearing sky. He looked out to the rusting cruise ship and then out to the eastern horizon.

Suddenly, there was a footfall on the stairs, Bella pricked up here ears as Drew's heart started racing. He turned around to see Rose appearing at the top of the stairwell.

"Rose, once again you have managed to scare the hell out of me."

"Sorry, Drew," she said sincerely. She was holding a sheathed army officer's sword in her hands. "I found this with Major Nate's things. I think he would have wanted you to have it."

Drew took the sword from Rose and unsheathed it in the moonlight. Starlight glinted off of the polished blade. Sheathing it, he fastened it at his hip, adjacent to Jack's 1911.

"He was a great man, Rose."

"I know."

The two of them stood side by side looking out over the ocean in silence.

"You did something incredible last night Rose," Drew started. "I know you had to make some heavy decisions, ones that may stay with you. I want to tell you that I will always stand by those choices that you made. You saved lives and saved heartache."

"If you're worried about me shooting Mr. Faulkner you shouldn't be. He just didn't need to say another word," Rose responded.

"You're just as straight to the point as Shark, that's for sure," Drew said, smiling.

"Do you think he is out there?" Rose asked.

"I would like to believe that he is, Rose. It still is difficult though after what we saw today." Drew said.

"How about the Ritz-Carlton, do you think that the same guys that came here shot that place up as well?"

"That would probably be my guess. Faulkner probably called ahead to that Carlos guy and told them about the survivors there. The other night he was asking about a possible rescue and was probably worried that we could gain more people. That's probably why he pulled the plug on us so soon."

"I'm not sure if you have noticed but there are not as many of them, mostly just Walkers now," Rose said, turning and looking out over the fort to the infected beyond.

"There will be more," Drew assured her.

They remained silent for a moment.

"So Drew, now that your big man in charge, what is your plan?" Rose asked.

Drew looked out over the fort and then down at Rose.

"We are going to take back this island."

Looking up at him she smiled with her sarcastic teenage grin.

"I guess I'm going to need that bigger gun."